DARK CITADEL

Masters of the Shadowlands: 2

CHERISE SINCLAIR

VanScoy Publishing Group

Dark Citadel

ISBN 978-1-947219-46-5

Published by VanScoy Publishing Group

Cover Artist: Christine M. Griffin

TO MY READERS

The books I write are fiction, not reality, and as in most romantic fiction, the romance is compressed into a very, very short time period.

You, my darlings, live in the real world, and I want you to take a little more time in your relationships. Good Doms don't grow on trees, and there are some strange people out there. So while you're looking for that special Dom, please, be careful.

When you find him, realize he can't read your mind. Yes, frightening as it might be, you're going to have to open up and talk to him. And you listen to him, in return. Share your hopes and fears, what you want from him, what scares you spitless. Okay, he may try to push your boundaries a little —he's a Dom, after all—but you will have your safe word. You will have a safe word, am I clear? Use protection. Have a back-up person. Communicate.

Remember: safe, sane, and consensual.

Know that I'm hoping you find that special, loving person who will understand your needs and hold you close.

And while you're looking or even if you have already found your dear-heart, come and hang out with the Masters of the Shadowlands.

Love,

Cherise

CHAPTER ONE

The massive stone building loomed over the extensive grounds like a forbidding castle in some gothic novel. *Club Shadowlands*. Kari Wagner shook her head at the intimidating sight, at the thought of what the evening might hold.

Beginners lessons at a private BDSM club. She'd gone insane. Really. Her mind had rotted completely away. Teaching high school, that's what had caused her lapse in sanity. All those teenagers...

Her date, Brian—or Buck, as he liked to be called—grabbed Kari's arm and pulled her through the front door. She slipped a little, and his grip hardened. "Damn, you're slow."

In the small entry room, a huge security guard stood behind a table, looking so ogrelike he was almost cute. "Good evening, sir, miss."

"Good evening." Kari closed her mouth before she called him Shrek.

He held out his hand. "Papers, please?"

As Buck handed over the doctor's certificates and money, Kari eased her arm away. She'd been attracted to his authoritative personality—so different from the usual men she dated—but he'd never been rough before. Then again, he didn't know how to do this domination stuff any more than she did.

The guard finished looking at the papers and handed them off to another man before saying, "I'll take your jacket, sir. And miss? Please leave your shoes with me now."

"My shoes?" After a glance at the guy to see if he was serious—he was—Kari slipped off her orange sneakers.

The guard patiently kept his hand outstretched until she handed over her Tigger-decorated socks also. A little snort of laughter escaped him. "Thank you, miss."

Buck's pale brows drew together at the sight of the socks. "What the hell are you wearing?"

Kari glanced down at her ankle-length denim dress. "Sorry. It was parent-teacher day, and my last set of parents arrived a half hour late. I didn't have time to go home and change."

"Honestly, Kari, you dress like a five-year-old." He straightened the lapels of his black suit.

"Well, I used to teach kindergarten after all." She laughed. "But my high-school students like my clothes too." And some thought she was terminally strange. But even if she'd had time to change, what would she have worn to a BDSM club? Some weird lacy corset thing? Surely they'd dated long enough for him to know her better than that.

"Well, folks, have a pleasant evening." Smiling, the guard pointed them toward a door on the right wall.

Wait a minute. Kari frowned at her bare feet, then looked at the man. "Excuse me, but why is Buck allowed to keep his shoes on?"

The guard blinked. "Did I make a mistake? Which one of you is the Dom or Domme?"

"I am." Buck gave her a disgusted look. "Just be quiet, Kari. Don't talk at all."

She bit back her first response—and the second—and settled for a nod. Buck might look like Prince Charming—tall, slim, blond—but his manners needed a little work. Still, she should give him a break. If he wasn't Mr. Perfect Dominating Man, she wasn't exactly a ten on the Gorgeous Submissive Woman scale, right? In fact, considering her conservative upbringing, this whole evening was probably doomed to failure.

Before they reached the door, Buck yanked her to his side, his fingers digging into her skin. "There will be other Doms here and other beginners. Remember you're with me. Don't talk to anyone else. Don't look at anyone else."

"Got it. Now let go of me." With an exasperated sigh, she pried his hand from her arm, then followed him into a large office with lush dark brown carpeting and creamy white walls. An antique desk and office equipment took up the far side of the room. In the right corner, several big men and two women, all dressed in gold-trimmed leather clothing, eyed her and Buck before returning to their quiet conversations.

The center of the room held a sitting area occupied by two men. One was a tall, broad-shouldered man with silvering dark hair wearing European-tailored black slacks and a black silk shirt. His dark gray eyes had focused on her and Buck the minute they walked through the door. Now, he tilted his head toward the couch across from him.

"That's got to be Master Z," Buck hissed as they crossed the room. "All this is his. You watch your mouth and don't speak unless I give you permission."

She did exactly that, closing her mouth over her impulse to tell him where to go. He meant well, and she wasn't going to leave before she found out more about this bondage stuff and why it excited her so much.

In black leathers, the other man looked downright dangerous: hard-faced with an equally hard body, open vest stretching over broad shoulders. Black hair slightly curling to the nape of his neck, potent brown eyes, the shadow of a beard along a stern jaw. If Buck was the golden prince, this man was the dark one.

When the men rose, Kari froze, feeling like a mouse confronted by lions. Mouth dry, she managed to move forward and smile.

"Buck," the gray-eyed one said in a smooth, deep voice. "Welcome to the Shadowlands. I am Master Z." He shook hands with Buck and then Kari. His warm hand engulfed her cold fingers as he studied her for a moment. "Welcome, Kari."

She opened her mouth, remembered not to speak, and smiled instead.

Master Z nodded to the other man. "This is Master Dan."

The man nodded, shook hands with Buck, and then took Kari's hand, his grip much gentler than she'd expected. When she looked up, his dark brown eyes trapped hers. He didn't leer or do anything other than look at her, yet she felt a flush rise into her face. She pulled her hand back and looked down. She could still feel his penetrating gaze.

"Please be seated," Master Z said. He waited for everyone to sit, then resumed his seat. He tapped the coffee table where their medical records and questionnaires were spread. "Your papers are in order. You're both free of any disease."

He glanced at her and Buck. "The rules of the Shadowlands are simple. Don't touch anything or anyone that doesn't belong to you without permission. Do not interfere in someone else's scene. The equipment is here for your use, and after your introductory class tonight, there are private rooms upstairs, also for your use." He nodded to the men in the corner. "Dungeon monitors—DMs—supervise activities and are available to answer questions or even to help as needed. Watch for the gold trim or an orange badge."

His gaze turned to Kari. "Here at the Shadowlands, use the term 'Master' for those in authority over you: me, the DMs, and possibly, your Dom. When in doubt, address any Dom as Sir or Ma'am."

"I understand. Thank you," she said without thinking and winced at Buck's glare.

Dan Sawyer half listened to Master Z while he sized up the two people who would be in his charge. The bland-faced man with pale blond hair and blue eyes. About five-eleven and a lanky one-seventy in a black suit. He had a narrow mouth with more frown lines than laugh lines and checked his date frequently as if afraid she'd disappear.

The woman wasn't beautiful, but compellingly pretty. Midtwenties. Wide blue eyes and hair the rich brown color of Guinness. A soft pink mouth bracketed by faint lines, showing she knew how to laugh and did it often. She was little, about five-four, and definitely not slender. Her long dress couldn't conceal her very lush curves despite being buttoned right up to the top.

Interesting choice of attire for the club. Was she modest? Probably. He studied the way she'd pulled her hair into a tight French braid. Modest *and* conservative. Huh.

He rubbed his chin and studied her further. Had she wanted to be in a BDSM club, or had her date dragged her? Maybe he had, considering the way she was rubbing her arm.

Shaking his head, Dan leaned back in his chair. Looked like this couple would bear watching.

She'd be a pleasure to watch. To see her tremble. To see the helpless need in those big eyes. To see... He set his imagination aside. Wherever those thoughts had come from, they were out of place. He was a teacher tonight.

A roar of laughter from the corner caught his attention, and he glanced at the other DMs for beginners' nights. All had been Dominants for years, all trustworthy men and women. Some with their own submissives, some, like Dan, without. A few were looking for a new sub to train. Dan wasn't.

There were plenty of subs begging for his use, and he

frequently enjoyed one for an evening, but his interest in long-term commitments had died with his wife three years ago. No one could replace his Marion.

"Then you're ready to start." Master Z's voice broke into Dan's thoughts.

The lecture was over; time to get the puppies moving. Dan rose. "Come with me. I'll show you around the club and answer questions until your class begins."

And like puppies, they followed him across the room, obediently at first. Then Dan heard the man whispering and turned. He caught a few words: "...stay right beside...guys trying to grab themselves a woman...saw how he looked at you. You belong to me...I'm in charge."

"Uh-huh." The woman rolled her eyes and tried to move away.

Buck grabbed her arm hard enough that she winced. His voice rose. "Are you listening to me?"

Having once been married, Dan could have told him those were fighting words.

And yes, Kari's face turned pink with anger. She yanked her arm away and stepped back. "Yes, I'm listening, and I don't like what I hear. I'm going home."

Buck's face darkened. "Don't be childish. You knew this was going to—"

She spun on her heel, headed for the door.

He grabbed her wrist. "Look, honey, I'm sorry. Maybe I—"

"Let me go!" She tried to pry his hand off and failed.

Oh, hell, Dan thought. The guy apparently didn't understand the basic *fuck off!* she'd put so politely.

"Let her go." Dan set his hand on the wannabe Dom's shoulder, tightening his fingers until the man flinched and released her.

"If she doesn't want to continue, you can't force her," Dan said. He glanced at the girl. "Kari, do you want to leave?"

"Yes. I do," she said. From the pissed-off look in her big blue eyes, she'd crossed the dude off her date list. *Smart move, sweetie*. Did she have a ride home? "Did you come together or—"

"Separately," she said.

"Then I'll walk you to your car." And prevent any altercations in the parking lot. "Buck, if you want to continue, go on in."

The man stood there for a minute, then scowled at his date. "Fine. I'm going to take the class since I already put out the money. I'll call you later, and we'll talk. I would have taken good care of you. You're not being reasonable at all." Straightening his suit coat, he headed for the door to the main club room.

"Well, then." Dan looked down at his charge. She was rubbing her arm again. "Are you all right, sweetheart?"

Startled, she looked up and he caught his breath at the hint of pain in her eyes, at the vulnerability. The *need*. His body responded as if she'd been stripped and tied to his bed. *Damn*.

"Um. Yes, thank you very much. I'm sorry about this," she said, her voice was melodic, a little husky. And so very polite. What would it take to break through the politeness to the woman beneath?

"No problem." He nodded toward the front door.

But as they passed the sitting area, Z lifted a hand, stopping them. "Kari, sit down, please."

She took a seat and folded her hands in her lap, all prim and proper except for the pink toes peeking out from under her dress.

"I see you and your date have parted ways," Z said. "But you obviously had an interest in this lifestyle or you would not be here. Am I correct?"

Her eyes dropped, and she nodded slightly.

"Excellent." Master Z continued, "Since that is the case, Master Dan, could you secure her a drink and see if she would like to continue tonight's class with you?"

The woman's head jerked up. "Continue? But..."

Z's glance at Dan was filled with amusement before he said, "Indeed, continue. Master Dan has far more experience and is far more gentle than your...other choice." Z's voice lowered, commanded, "Look at him now."

Instant compliance. *Submissive. Innocent. Temptingly lovely.* Before he could stop himself, Dan held his hand out. "We'll go discuss it, Kari. Come."

Again, that appealing obedience.

As he curled his fingers around the cold little hand, he could only think about the next time he would order her to come. With his fingers inside her and his mouth on her clit, yes, she would most surely come.

CHAPTER TWO

Oh God, what was she doing?

The man's grasp enfolded her hand. *Master Dan*. She didn't even know his last name.

They crossed the room, heading toward a heavy wooden door. She halted abruptly.

"Kari?"

She looked up. Good grief, he was even bigger than Buck. Somewhere over six feet, but when you're short, anything over six feet was hard to judge. His shoulders were beyond broad. Like the other men in the room, his gold-trimmed black leather vest had nothing under it. Well, nothing except muscles and more muscles and a sprinkling of black chest hair.

His biceps bulged, and his forearms appeared almost as thick. The leathers he wore for pants were—wow, really tight.

When her gaze managed to move back up to his face, he smiled, laugh lines crinkling around his eyes. Her face heated, and she knew her pale skin reddened.

"You're allowed to look, sweetheart," he murmured, running a finger down her hot cheek. "I enjoy having your eyes on me."

His eyes were a dark, dark brown, his face tanned and hard

looking until he smiled. But when he didn't... She remembered the hard look on his face when he had grabbed Buck. She bit her lip. Go home, she told herself. Now.

He started to push the door open.

"No. Wait, please." She held up her hand. "If it wouldn't inconvenience you, might I take a minute to think?"

"Take all the time you need." Crossing his arms, he leaned one shoulder against the wall, amusement in his eyes.

Just standing here beside him wasn't going to work. Shoot, even Madame Curie wouldn't be able to think with that man looking at her. Kari turned her back and paced across the room.

Stay or not? That was the basic question for tonight. So check the facts.

If she simply went home, nothing would change. Her life would go on. She'd never know if she might have learned something that would make a difference in her sex life. Nothing else had. How many relationships had failed due to her lack of interest in sex? She'd thought her basic personality or body created the problem. But the excitement she felt hearing about domination—heck, just the word itself—had been amazing. A revelation in a way.

She could definitely get aroused.

But this BDSM stuff appeared very, very strange. Kinky. And she wasn't a kinky person in the least. Shoot, the school nuns had used her as an example of model behavior. "*Why can't you be more like Kari? She's polite. She follows the rules.*"

Well, following the rules in the bedroom wasn't working too well for her, now was it?

She reached the end of the room and turned around. Master Dan hadn't moved, his patience apparently inexhaustible. Nonetheless, she needed to figure this out, pros and cons, and reach a decision.

In the Go Home column: First, she didn't know nearly enough about this stuff. She scowled as she paced back. Her home computer had died last month—stupid technology—and she couldn't afford to replace it yet. She sure couldn't research BDSM on the school computer. So she only knew the tidbits Buck had doled out. Her mouth tightened. She *hated* being ignorant.

Second: She didn't know this man at all. How dangerous was that? She could just imagine all her friends and family mourning around her grave. The tombstone would read *Kari Wagner, Died of Sheer Stupidity*.

In the Stay Here column: It would be almost as bad to have her grave marker read *Died of Terminal Bedroom Boredom*. Unmarried and childless. There was a darned good reason she wanted to try this stuff, after all.

As for knowing the man? She glanced at Master Z. The owner had leaned back in his chair, fingers steepled, watching her pace. He was no dummy, and he'd basically recommended Master Dan.

And Master Dan sure wasn't anything like Buck. She pursed her lips. She considered that a major bonus, right there.

What about being ignorant? Well, she might be, but she had a feeling that Master Dan knew *all* about the subject of domination.

She stopped in front of the door to the bar, could hear the sounds of classical music and muted conversation. If she left now, she would never have the courage to return. Her head said no. Her heart said go for it.

Master Dan straightened.

She placed her hand in his. Go it was.

"Nervous?" he asked softly.

"A bit." No point in hiding the truth. Considering her heart was trying to pound through her chest, he could probably hear the noise.

"Let me make it easier. Right now, all we will do is go into the club room and talk. Can you trust me that far?"

Just talk in a bar. She could handle that. "Okay. The bar."

"Good girl." His eyes softened.

Opening the door, he escorted her through, setting a warm hand low on her back.

Once inside, Kari paused to look around. The huge room boasted a circular bar in the center and wrought iron circular stairs in the corners. Groups of plants sectioned the tables and overstuffed couches into secluded sitting areas. Flickering wall sconces and glass chandeliers hanging from low rafters provided shadowy light and made the hardwood floor gleam.

A scattering of people occupied the couches and bar stools. To Kari's relief, no one was doing weird things or having sex on the floor. Leathers, latex, and skimpy dresses seemed the attire of choice—nothing too outlandish.

He followed her gaze. "Beginners tend to dress conservatively. You'll see a big difference when the regular club members are here on Saturday."

As they crossed the room, Kari spotted Buck at the bar. Her step faltered.

He noticed her, and his face lit up. Then he saw Master Dan with his arm around her, and his mouth compressed so hard his lips disappeared.

To her relief, he didn't approach. She would hate to be the cause of a scene or be the center of attention.

Without speaking, Master Dan slid his hand up to her waist and moved her closer, his nearness comforting.

Once past the bar, he found an unoccupied sitting area. Taking the very center of the couch, he pulled her down beside him. He smelled of subtly dark cologne, of soap...of *man*. And she was way too close. She tried to shift away, only to realize he'd wedged her between him and the arm of the couch.

"Does it bother you to sit beside me?" he asked, leaning back and studying her. His leg against her thigh was hard, ungiving.

Did he expect her to be rude? "Um, no, of course not." Trying to ignore the feeling of being crowded, she tipped her foot up, wiggled her toes. Why was she barefoot anyway?

"Look at me." He put gentle fingers under her chin, forcing her to meet his level gaze.

"Kari, part of the adventure is being honest with each other. When I ask you a question, I want an honest answer, not a polite one." He smiled slightly. His fingers were warm as his thumb traced little circles on her cheek. "Let me show you what I'd like."

He pitched his voice a little higher and said, "Master Dan, when I realized I was between you and the couch arm, I felt trapped. Like I can't retreat if I want to." His voice returned to its natural subterranean deepness. "Is that about right?"

How did he know that?

He kept watching her with those intent eyes, and each stroke of his thumb across her skin left heat in its wake. He lifted his dark brows. "Kari?"

"Yes," she said almost inaudibly. "That's how I feel." The admission left her feeling as if she'd undressed in front of him, and she tried to look away. He tipped her head back, let her see the pleasure on his face.

"Good girl. I can tell that wasn't easy for you." He brushed a kiss across her lips.

Her lips tingled although the touch had been fleeting, a tiny hint of pleasure.

Dan studied the little newbie. Nervous as a burglar who'd tripped an alarm. And so polite. Her hands lay in her lap, laced together.

"May I ask you some questions?" He massaged her cold little fingers as he waited for her reply.

"Of course. May I ask questions also?" She fidgeted. He watched her fidget. His deliberate intrusion into her personal space definitely set her off balance.

"I hope you will since that's my job tonight, being an instructor. So what do you do when you're not in a wicked house of sin?"

"I'm a—" She hesitated, stiffening a little.

Smart girl, not blurting out too much personal information. Caution wasn't a bad thing. "Ah. Never mind that. Why don't you tell me about the assh—about Buck? I'm assuming he's not your husband."

"No!" Obviously horrified, she frowned at him. "I wouldn't have gone with you if I were married."

"Good to hear. Just a boyfriend, then?" And hadn't the man looked steamed there at the bar. Dan automatically checked his surroundings. All clear.

"I was dating him." She studied her fingers. "He's usually a nice man. I'm not sure why he was like that tonight."

The idea of dominance brought out more than just true Dominants. Perverts, control freaks, and general assholes were plentiful. "You need to be careful about who you trust when you're getting into any kind of power exchange. That's why the class is restricted to this room tonight. No one goes anywhere private." He put his arm across her shoulders, pulling her closer. Curves and softness. Delightful. "Have you ever been married?"

"No. Engaged once, but it didn't work out." The muscles around her eyes tightened...a past hurt? Before he could quiz her, she asked hastily, "How about you? Are you married or involved?"

The unexpected question stabbed through him, and he forced his voice to stay even. "No. My wife died a few years ago. A car accident."

"I'm so sorry." She laid her hand on his cheek. "Do you have children?"

He shook his head. "She wanted to wait. She said she was having too much fun to want to slow down." At times, he could be grateful he wasn't responsible for a child; other times, he ached for someone to love.

"I'm sorry," she repeated.

"Thank you." Her sympathy touched him inside, lightened the heavy feeling in his gut. He took her hand and pressed a kiss to the center.

She smiled at him, her eyes gentle...and pulled her hand back.

Her retreat returned him to the present. So the little miss might be shy, but not when someone needed comfort.

"Um—Mas—"

"So many worries. If 'Master Dan' feels awkward, call me Sir. Any other designation here will get you in trouble."

She frowned. "All right, but—"

He interrupted, taking her hand. "So, Kari. We get a variety of people on beginners' nights. Some have used bondage and such at home, sometimes for years. Do you have any experience at all?"

"Not really. I...we...Buck wanted to tie my hands, and I wouldn't let him." Her muscles tensed, and she tugged at her hand. "I probably don't belong here. Not really. I'm not—"

He chuckled but didn't release her hand or move his arm from her shoulders. "You know, if someone like Buck tried to tie me up, I'd run for the hills. All that shows is your body has better taste in men than your mind."

She blinked. Relaxed a little.

"What does your body say about being with me?" he asked. "Do you feel safe?"

Glancing away from him, she considered, and her brows drew together. "Pretty much. Yes." She sounded surprised.

"All right then. Now tell me about your fiancé. Did you two try anything?"

Her lips curved up. "Oh, no. The thought would have appalled him."

He traced a finger over her plump lips, and her gaze darted to him. "So no experience at all. Why are you here?"

She looked down, pulled in a long breath, and raised those gorgeous eyes back to his. "Buck told me about domination and bondage, and I didn't realize real people do...it. I've never been that interested in sex, but when I heard about this, I was..."

"Turned on?"

She nodded. "But honestly, I don't think this will work for me. I'm very... I'm not the type of person who—"

"You're modest. Polite. Obey the rules."

Relief at being understood showed in her eyes. "Yes. Exactly. My father was quite devout and very strict with my sister and me. Catholic girls' school, no dating in high school, no makeup. She rebelled; I was the good daughter." She gave him a sidelong look. "I'm very repressed."

He laughed. Not so repressed that she'd lost her sense of humor. Still, that explained a lot. Dan fingered her tight French braid, glanced at the dress buttoned to her neck. She wouldn't find this easy.

"So you see, I'm probably wasting your time. I'm very sorry."

Now he knew about her background, he thought she'd been brave just to come here. Should he let her go? He thought about the way her eyes had heated at just a simple command. "Let's talk a little longer and see."

Her foot pointed to the door, but her fingers still gripped his hand. She wanted and didn't want. Did she have any idea how that type of dichotomy could entice a Dom?

"All right." She raised her chin.

"All right," he echoed. "We've established you have no experience. How about fantasies?"

CHAPTER THREE

Kari felt herself turn red.

"Well, she has fantasies." He grinned. "Good. A gorgeous barbarian chasing you down and taking you against your will? Have you had that one?"

"I—" She bit her lower lip. Was she wearing an I-have-kinky-dreams brand or something?

"I would enjoy chasing you; I wonder if you'd enjoy being caught?" His hand cupped her cheek, turning her head so he could kiss her. Ever so lightly, his mouth teased hers, coaxing her to respond. He had firm lips, but smooth, and she moved closer, wanting more. He traced her lips with his tongue, nibbled on her bottom lip, and when she opened for him, he swept inside, sending her senses reeling.

When he pulled back, her fingers were clamped on his upper arms. She fought to catch her breath. A furnace seemed to have started in her body. God, she wanted to kiss him some more.

He smiled and traced her wet lips with his finger. "Save our place," he whispered.

Kari blinked, realized a woman stood beside the couch, her

gaze on the floor. She wore a red latex corset, a short black skirt, and wrist cuffs. How long had she been standing there?

"Tabitha."

"Master Dan, may I bring you and your companion something to drink?"

"Kari, what would you like? No, let me see how close I can get." He studied her, and a crease appeared in his cheek with his smile. "It would have to be like you. Sweet. Not exotic, but straightforward. Honest. A screwdriver or perhaps rum and Coke?"

Her jaw dropped. "Rum and Diet Coke. How did you know?"

He nodded at Tabitha, and the young woman disappeared. "Yes, let's talk about that. Part of a Dominant-submissive relationship is—" His eyes glinted with amusement. "Ah, even the words make you blush. Such a lovely pink."

And she could feel her face turning redder with the compliment, darn him. She'd taken her turn at teaching sex education classes and never blushed once. Why now?

"Dominant. Submissive," he said clearly. "Say the words for me, Kari."

Well, that wasn't asking too much, considering where she was. "Dominant. Submissive," she said, managing to speak a little louder than a whisper—maybe not much.

His smile was like a reward. "Good. Shall I give you a harder assignment? *I* am a *Dominant*." He tilted his head at her to finish.

"I—I—" But she wasn't. Not really... Was she? It was one thing to be thinking about being, well, *controlled* in bed, and quite another to apply an actual label to herself. Labels had meaning. And made everything far too real. This was just supposed to be... an *experiment*.

"Mmmph, that *is* a hard admission, not one you are ready for. Let's put a limit on it then. For the next hour, until nine o'clock, I am a Dominant."

She could do an hour. In fact, that's exactly what she wanted to do. "For the next hour, until nine o'clock, I am a submissive," she said firmly.

And she shivered.

That smile again. "Brave girl."

Tabitha arrived with their drinks, set them on the table quietly, and departed without a word. "Is she a submissive?"

He handed over her drink, took his. "Yes. In training here."

Training. You had to train to be ordered around?

The skin around his eyes crinkled with humor. "You're here for three evenings of classes." He stroked his knuckles along her jaw. "Training is for those wanting to go deeper into the lifestyle, not something you need to worry about."

"Okay. Good." She sipped her drink, blinked at the strength, and sipped again. "How many people end up drunk?"

"None." He drank some of his, clear as water, and set it back on the table. "Master Z limits everyone to two drinks."

Now how could they enforce that? Then she remembered how Sir's big hand had gripped Buck's shoulder, and she felt a tickle of laughter. Enforcement obviously wasn't a problem. And she should pay for her own drink. She fumbled at the pocket of her dress where she'd tucked her key and some money. "The barmaid didn't say what my rum and Coke cost."

"No cost. Drinks are included in membership fees, or for you, the price of the class."

Oh. She put her hands back in her lap. "What happens now?"

"Now we simply talk about what suits your needs."

She stared down into her drink, watching the bubbles. His silence had her looking up, right into his observant eyes.

"Needs is another word that bothers you," he said. "Talking about sex isn't something you do, is it?"

What, did he have some sort of view into her head? "It wasn't an acceptable topic of conversation when I was growing up, no." Her father could expound for hours on purity and innocence without ever saying the sex word.

"Mmmph, in that case, let me run through some options, and we'll take it from there."

Options sounded good. Were there options that were the equivalent of sticking one toe in the water? She took another sip of her drink. "All right."

"I have one request first."

A request in this place might involve just about anything. She eyed him warily. Nodded.

"Can I get you to sit on my lap while we talk?" He ran a finger over her lower lip, slowly, and she grew aware of how soft her own lips were. His mouth curved up in a wicked smile. "I promise not to put my hands anywhere you don't want them."

"But why would I sit on your lap?"

"Sweetheart, it will make it easier for you; sex isn't something to be discussed at arm's length, now is it?"

Sex. With him. She might consider this evening an experiment, but sex wasn't that way. It was personal. He'd be touching her. Intimately. But she wanted this; she really did. "All right."

She set her drink on the table and rose to her feet, smoothing her dress down. He slid into her place. Reclining back against the armrest, he put his legs up and pulled her into his lap.

With her feet still on the floor, she sat stiffly until he laughed and pulled her down against his chest, her head in the hollow of his shoulder. Sit on his lap? This was more like snuggling...and pretty nice. After a moment, she let her hand rest on his bare chest where the vest had fallen away. She ruffled the crisp hair, tracing her fingers over the hard contours of his chest. He was so darned big, she actually felt tiny next to him—well, on top of him—like her weight was nothing to him.

His voice rumbled through his chest. "There we go. You fit into my arms very nicely—a nice, soft armful."

His obvious enjoyment warmed her, made her feel feminine and attractive, something she'd been missing for a while now. For two years, actually, since Curt had left her for some hot, skinny artist.

"What was that thought?" Dan asked. She could feel his fingers in her hair, unpinning the French braid.

"Noth—"

"Kari."

She could hear the warning in his voice, and somehow she didn't want to disappoint him. "I was thinking about my ex-fiancé."

"And?"

"And how fat and frigid he made me feel, okay?" she snapped and tried to sit up, but he tucked an arm across her waist and held her in place. Easily.

"Stay here, little one." He laughed, a low, growling sound. "You have a temper buried under all that politeness. I wonder what else is buried down there."

"I'm sorry." He'd only been nice to her, and she'd lashed out.

"I'm not. You know, with both the temper and the worries about your size, you remind me of Z's sub. Personally, I like women with some padding. I like lush." He stroked up to just under her breasts, and she froze.

"And curvy." He ran his hand across her hip, squeezed her bottom, continued down her thigh. Everywhere his hand touched, her skin wakened like spring after a hard winter, and warmth washed through her.

"You have the loveliest fair skin," he murmured, trailing his fingers down her arm. "Soft and creamy, and those pillowy lips of yours would tempt an angel to sin. I'm no angel." His hand tangled in her loose hair, tipping her head back, and his mouth settled on hers. His lips were firm, demanding, opening hers and taking possession without mercy.

When he pulled back, she was breathing hard, her hand fisted in his vest. God, the man could kiss.

"And only an idiot would call you cold," he murmured. "Now,

back to business. First of all, I need to find out what kind of a submissive you might be. I think I know, but let's be sure."

"Submissives come in different types?" How could she know so little? When she got home, she was going to take a hammer to that stupid dead computer. "I'm afraid I don't know what you're talking about. Can we try multiple choice?"

He laughed. "All right. *A:* You want to serve a master, making him meals, doing whatever he wants, around the house or in bed. *B:* You want to play a role for a short time, be a schoolgirl or a secretary, but you'd set up your own rules with your top—ah, the person in charge. *C:* You want to give up control for sex but not especially for anything else. *D:* You like pain and want someone to deal it out."

That was quite a list. "People really want all those different things?"

"Oh, definitely. That was just the short list." He tugged on her hair. "Give me a letter, sweetheart."

Well, she knew what she wanted. Why the heck couldn't she be as blasé about sex as her friends were? She wet her lips. "*C.* We—I came here—" She sighed. "*C.*"

"Good enough," he said easily. "Choice *C* for sex."

At least he hadn't jumped up and yelled, *You want what?* in horror. She realized her fingernails were digging into his side and made her hand relax.

Taking hold of her hips, he moved her lower on his lap and slid his arm tighter around her until his hand settled under her breasts. His other hand stroked her neck, her collarbone. She sighed in pleasure, squirming a little to get even closer, and froze when she realized what she was squirming on. He was not only hard; he was huge.

"Sorry," she whispered.

"Don't be sorry about giving someone pleasure, sweetling." His fingers played with her hair that spilled down her front. Somehow several buttons on her dress had come undone, and his hand dropped to rest on the beginning swell of her breast with his other hand just below. One above, one below, like he was holding her breasts captive between the two. Why did that seem erotic?

"How do you feel about being told what to do in bed?"

She caught her breath as the image sent a wave of heat through her. "Um."

But he didn't wait for her answer, just murmured, "That's a go."

A second later, he moved his hand from below her breasts and slid it into her dress where more buttons had come undone. His hand settled back to where it had been before, only now his warm palm lay directly on her naked skin, grazing the lower edge of her breasts. She stiffened and then forced herself to relax. She was here for sex, right?

"Some people like being tied down, kept from moving while their partner pleasures them."

She managed not to squeak.

"Your body likes that idea."

Another pause and she realized she was rubbing her thighs together and stopped immediately. *Tied* up for sex. Being ordered around was one thing, but restrained with ropes or handcuffs? Too much. She hadn't liked the idea at all when Buck had tried it. "No," she said shakily. "I think you're wrong."

"Let's see." He touched his lips to hers, kissed her sweetly, thoroughly, his tongue tangling with hers. When he drew back, she smiled with pleasure.

"That's called vanilla sex," he murmured.

Suddenly he gripped her wrists with hard hands, holding her so she couldn't move. "And this is nonvanilla sex." He took her mouth again, plunging deeply, possessing her ruthlessly. When she tried to move, his grip tightened on her arms, holding her in place.

She couldn't *move*. Every nerve in her body shocked to life as if lightning struck her. Arousal seared through her. She bit back a moan.

He released her, quirking a cynical eyebrow.

Deep inside, her body shook like a palm tree in a tropical storm. What was happening to her? She pulled in a breath. "That didn't..." Her voice trailed off. She was lying to herself and to him. "You're right."

"I like your honesty." Wrapping his arms around her again, he stroked her back. Her cheek rested on his bare chest. His heart beat in a slow, relaxing rhythm, and her own pulse slowed as the claws of desire unhooked from her.

"On your last night, you'll have to take a look at the costumes the members wear," he said conversationally. It's pretty amazing some of the things people put on. Of course, since it's beginners' night, tonight's attire is pretty sedate." As he talked, he slid one hand into her dress again, nestling up against her breasts, the other resuming its place just under her collarbone.

"You know, some people like a little pain now and then: spanking, pinching, tiny punishments."

It was as if he was having this conversation with himself, except the images he put into her head were just... A man spanking her bare bottom? *Jeez, no.* And yet, she actually felt herself dampen.

"Mmm-hmm, yes, I think you'll need a little reprimand now and then."

Her breath hitched. He wouldn't really, now would he?

He rubbed his chin against the top of her head. "You smell good, little sub. Like soap and flowers and...woman. And your hair is as long and silky as any man could want."

Okay, she'd just lie here all night, snuggled into his naked chest, and let him talk to her with that low, low voice. Listening to him was better than having sex with—with anyone she'd ever been with before.

"You know, some people like more pain: being whipped hard, pins inserted under their skin, hot wax dripped on them."

She froze. That... He wouldn't. She shoved against his chest, tried to get free.

"No, that's not for you. Definitely not."

Body stiff, she tried to slide off him.

One arm held her tight against him as his other hand stroked her hair as if he were petting a cat, settling her down. "Truthfully, Kari, I don't like the hardcore S and M either. Real pain doesn't turn me on, and I can see you feel the same."

She took a breath and let herself relax. A little. "Do people really do that? Here?"

"Yes. You'll see some of that, maybe on Wednesday, definitely on Saturday. It's not something you need to do if you're not into it."

"Well, that's good. Thank you." He was so warm and his arms so comforting that when he tilted her head back for another kiss, she didn't resist at all.

Pulling back, he looked her in the eyes and said, "If anytime, anything I do or we do goes beyond what you can stand, then you say 'red,' and everything stops. That's your safe word, sweetheart. Red. Make sense?"

Cool. She could stop everything when she wanted. The sense of relief mingled with confusion. That didn't seem like she was giving up much control.

He kissed her again, and his big hand slid up to cover her breast, his thumb brushing across her nipple. Each touch sent zings of intense sensation spearing through her until she was squirming again.

"Kari, the safe word is for pain. Or something you absolutely can't stand. You use it for anything less, and the night is over. I pack you up, and you go home." His intent gaze trapped hers. "I am going to give you what you want, not what your mama told you is proper. I'm going to push your limits, sweetie."

He nuzzled her until his lips were against her ear. "And you're going to scream as you come over and over again."

She gasped, could feel her nipples harden, and so could he, considering his hand was right there on her breast. He chuckled, sucked on her earlobe, and sent chills chasing across her skin.

"Ahem." Behind them, a woman cleared her throat. Kari jerked to a sitting position, embarrassed at her behavior in public. What had she been thinking?

A DM in a gold-trimmed black bustier and black latex leggings stood by the couch. "Sorry to interrupt," she said, her lips curving up.

Sir sighed. "Olivia. You, as always, have a crappy sense of timing. What?"

"Z said you are to participate in the newbie class. Both of you. Raoul's waiting for you."

"Well, hell. We'll be there."

Sir looked at Kari. "Up you go," he said briskly, pushing her to her feet. "You'll enjoy this, I think. At least the last part of the class." He buttoned her dress, his fingers sliding into the gaps, teasing her sensitive skin, making her regret the interruption.

When he was finished, he ran his knuckles across her breasts, up and down over her jutting nipples. He grinned and murmured, "Guess you're just cold, huh?"

She couldn't keep the laugh bottled up.

They joined the thirty-or-so beginners milling around at the end of the bar. To Kari's surprise, the couples included not only male-female, but also gays and lesbians. With one heterosexual couple, the *man* wore cuffs and a collar. So men could be submissive? Too strange.

Then a gleam of blond hair caught Kari's gaze, and her eyes met Buck's. Grinning, he started toward her and then spotted Master Dan. A scowl darkened his long face, but he stopped.

Even as Kari breathed a sigh of relief, guilt welled within her. She'd arrived with him; she should still be with him.

"All right, people, let's get started." The dungeon monitor teaching the class was an inch or two shorter than Sir, but so thickly muscled he looked like he could pick up her car without breaking a sweat. "Master Dan," he said. "I've got a shy crowd here, and I want to run through some basic bondage. Bring your sub up here."

What?

Sir's arm tightened, and he swept her along, despite her attempt at planting her feet. "Don't worry, sweetling. This is show-and-tell with all your clothes on and no sex."

Well, she *was* used to being in front of people, if teenage students counted as people, something she rather doubted. She shouldn't have a problem with this.

Master Dan nodded at the teacher. "Kari, this is Master Raoul."

She smiled at the man. Was she permitted to talk? Sir hadn't said.

As if he'd read her mind, he murmured, "Say hello, sweetheart."

"I'm very pleased to meet you," she said.

"Hello, Kari." The DM gave her a slow, appreciative look before frowning at Sir. "You always were Z's favorite."

"I know." Master Dan flashed a wicked grin. "So get moving. I have other things to do tonight."

"I bet." Turning back to the class, Master Raoul picked up a pair of metal handcuffs from the bar top. "This is the basic handcuff. Adequate, but if you get your sub excited and she yanks on them, she'll have nasty bruises for a few days. And it's easy to get them too tight. With these, as with all restraints, be sure you check the circulation frequently. Doms, this is a biggie: if you restrain someone, you never leave them alone."

He set the handcuffs down and held up leather wrist cuffs with buckles. "Much more comfortable and safer for circulation.

If your sub deserves it, you can even buy lined ones. Master Dan, if you would demonstrate."

Master Dan took the cuffs and held out one hand. "Give me your wrist, Kari," he said.

Her heart gave a hard thud, and she hesitated.

His eyebrows rose. "Now, Kari."

Her hand plopped into his before she'd come up with all the reasons she should say no.

He buckled first one, then the other cuff on, running a finger under to be certain they were snug but not tight. Pulling her wrists in front of her, he hooked the cuffs together. The commanding look in his eyes and the feel of his firm hands on her arms made her stomach quiver and heat pool in her lower half.

When he finished, he stepped back, studying her face. His lips curved in a hard smile.

Trying to ignore the dampness seeping between her thighs, she yanked at the cuffs. She definitely couldn't get free of them, but still, this wasn't all that scary. Her hands were in front of her; she could defend herself.

Master Raoul nodded. "Basic restraint. Hands in front, but not very intimidating. Leaves a lot of room for evasion. Dan?"

To Kari's shock, Master Dan set his hand on one breast, cupping her firmly. Even as a thrill rushed through her, she instinctively knocked his fingers off with her cuffed hands and glared at him.

"Not a very obedient sub you have there," Master Raoul commented dryly as the group laughed.

Oh, heavens, had she embarrassed him? She shouldn't have reacted without thinking. Kari risked a glance.

Although he didn't smile, his cheek creased, and his eyes were amused as he unclipped her wrists.

"Hands behind the back will help solve that little aggression problem," Master Raoul said.

Master Dan stepped behind Kari and clipped the cuffs

together at the small of her back. This time, she yanked at them unsuccessfully, and a shiver ran through her at the helpless feeling. With her hands behind her back, she could do nothing to—

"And as you see, your sub is much more manageable," Master Raoul said.

Master Dan's hard chest pressed against her back as he reached around her, one arm securing her waist. His other hand closed on her breast. She jumped, squeaked, and couldn't move, couldn't get free as he caressed her, his fingers sending erotic sensations swirling through her.

CHAPTER FOUR

Dan felt Kari's heart pound as his fingers stroked her full breasts. He could also feel the way her nipples tightened. Arousal flushed her neck. No question, the little miss was submissive.

But so new. Just as well she had no idea how much control it took to not open those tiny buttons, slide his hand under her bra, stroke her soft skin, and roll her nipples between his fingers. And that would be just the beginning. Bending her over one of the couches, exposing her ass, and—

"There's a small problem with this type of bondage, however," Master Raoul stated.

Wrenching his mind back to business, Dan responded to the cue. He scooped Kari off her feet, enjoying the tiny squeal she gave. Kneeling, he laid her on her back on the floor and straddled her thighs. Her eyes were huge as she stared up at him.

"As you can see, she's lying on her arms, an uncomfortable position for a sub, especially if you plan to be on top of her." Raoul grinned.

Dan rose and set Kari back on her feet. The deep breath of relief she took made him chuckle.

"Thank you, Kari and Master Dan," Raoul said. "Now someone may volunteer for the next demonstration, or I will pick two people myself." A middle-aged couple stepped forward, and Raoul talked them through leg restraints.

Dan put his arm around Kari, enjoying her tiny squirms as she tested the cuffs every few seconds.

"You can take these off now," she whispered, giving him an annoyed look.

Those flashes of temper could drive a Dom crazy thinking of the various enjoyable ways to punish them. Again, she was too new, no serious disciplining allowed. But since she was still frowning up at him, her mouth was perfectly positioned, and he didn't resist. Tightening his grip on her waist, he kissed her. After a second of resistance, her lips softened, and his tongue plunged inside. He took her mouth thoroughly, as he wished he could take the rest of her before the night ended. Her quivering response made his blood boil and his cock strain to be set free.

With a regretful sigh, he pulled back, moving to stand beside her. One hand rested on her shoulder, strategically placed to feel her body's responses to the rest of the toys Raoul brought out. By the time Raoul finished the lesson, every beginner Dom had restrained a sub in one way or another, and Dan had discovered Kari was turned on by leg restraints also. Good to know.

Now the single students paired off, and everyone wandered through the club to practice what they'd learned. With beginners locked out of the private rooms upstairs, he and Kari were stuck down here too.

He remembered a relatively isolated area, though, near the back of the room and well hidden behind a bunch of foliage. He beckoned to a trainee. "Sally, run over and put a RESERVED sign on the sitting area to the left of the theme rooms."

The trainee laughed as she shook her head in disapproval. "Shame on you. That's cheati—" She shut her mouth quickly, several words too late.

. . .

Kari frowned as the barmaid dropped to her knees before Master Dan. The pretty brunette looked mortified and a bit frightened as she whispered, "I'm sorry, Master Dan."

Master Dan's expression hardened into stone. "I've lost patience with your lack of control over your tongue. Show me your bands," he snapped.

Sally held out her arms. Each wrist held a narrow leather cuff wrapped with yellow, blue, and green ribbons.

"First, do as I asked. Then report to Master Cullen and inform him you are to be given to a DM for spanking and his use. Are my instructions clear?"

Sally's eyes widened, and her outstretched hands trembled. "Yes, Sir."

"Go."

After pushing to her feet, the brunette escaped, almost tripping in her haste to get away.

Kari stared up at Master Dan, horror chilling her body. "Did you just give her to a stranger? Just like that?"

He turned. The coldness disappeared from his expression as if it had never been. "Ah, Kari. Sally is another sub in training. This is part of her instruction."

"But a spanking? And...use?" She had a pretty good idea what *use* meant. Dear God. Kari stepped back. She really didn't know this man at all.

Her hands were still cuffed, she realized with a jolt of fear.

"Dan—oops—Master Dan, I mean." A pretty blonde in tight jeans and an emerald green, low-cut blouse hurried up. "Z wants you to join him for a few minutes if you could. Something about club membership."

"Of course." Master Dan turned to Kari, and she took another step back. His eyes narrowed before he turned to the blonde. "Jessica, I disciplined Sally for mouthing off, and now Kari's terrified. She's probably convinced I'm a white slave trader. Can you stay with her and reassure her while I'm gone?"

"Only if you'll agree to join us for supper next Friday."

"Works for me. Sure." Pinning Kari in place with a hard look, he closed the distance between them. He stroked a finger down her cheek, sending a thrill through her.

She swallowed hard, unable to look away from his penetrating gaze. The man had just scared her spitless, so why did his touch still make her all quivery inside?

He smiled as if he could feel her response. After unhooking her hands from behind her back, he strode off toward the front of the room. Tall, straight shouldered, gorgeous—and more frightening than Hannibal Lector. She was in way over her head here.

"Ready for some female company?" the blonde asked, following her gaze.

"I would be very grateful." Kari stuck a hand out. "I'm Kari, and what you'd call a newbie, I guess."

The woman took her hand, gave a strong squeeze. Like Sally, she wore leather cuffs. Fur-lined, but lacking any ribbons. "I'm Jessica, and I'm past newbie status, but I haven't been in the scene very long. Let's have a drink and talk."

The circular bar was nearly deserted with only two beginners hovering at one end, and three dungeon monitors at the other. Kari slid onto a wooden stool beside Jessica.

In the center, the giant bartender concocted a fancy drink, humming to the soft music of Pachelbel's "Canon." In dark brown leathers that matched his thick hair, he had a rough face of blunt angles and a solid jaw. After delivering the drink to a newbie, he sauntered over to Kari and Jessica.

Leaning a big arm on the bar top, he gave Kari a long, slow look that made heat rise in her cheeks. "Little subbie, do you want another rum and Diet Coke?"

Would speaking get her in the same kind of trouble as Sally? What were the darned rules in this place? "Just Coke, please."

He didn't yell at her. Instead, he turned to Jessica. "Margarita?"

"Yes, thank you, Master Cullen."

His laugh boomed through the bar. "So formal. Setting a good example for your friend?"

Jessica grinned.

Master Cullen set the drinks in front of them, gave Kari another of those *looks*, and left to take another order. Her face heated. Jeez. With a rueful smile, she glanced at Jessica. "I swear, I've spent most of my time here blushing. And sometimes I'm not even sure why."

Jessica laughed. "If you mean Cullen, some of the more powerful Doms can make you turn red just by looking at you."

"Well, no wonder then." This place was obviously littered with strong Doms. Her mind turned back to what had caused the worry gnawing away in her stomach. "Tell me about Sally. When she messed up, Master Dan gave her to some Dom—any Dom—to *use*. That seems like almost rape."

"But it's not." Jessica held up her wrist. "Did you see the ribbons on her cuffs?"

Kari nodded.

"They show what kind of activities a trainee is into. Red for serious sadomasochism, yellow for milder pain like spankings, blue for bondage, and green for sex. If she had a green ribbon, she was all right with being given to any Dom here."

"Oh." Wow. What would that be like, to be just handed over to someone? Kari took a hefty gulp of her drink, wondering if she should have had the rum.

"This place can be overwhelming. The first time I was here, I just wanted shelter during a storm. I didn't know it was a BDSM club. There was all this *stuff* going on." She rolled her eyes. "I got in so much trouble..."

Kari grinned. "Tell me more."

"Next class, I'll give you the full story. For now, how do I convince you that Master Dan's not a white slave trader?"

"Uh. It helps knowing he didn't do something that Sally wasn't expecting, I guess." Kari frowned. But now that he wasn't touching her, looking at her, she was starting to have second thoughts. Did she really want to continue? All the other beginners were off in dark corners practicing that bondage stuff, and Master Dan would be expecting to do that with her. And he wasn't any beginner. A little thrill ran through her at the thought of his big hands on her, and she squashed it down. "But I don't know him, and to let him tie me up or something seems insane."

"I understand completely. What can I tell you about him..." Jessica tapped a finger against her chin as she thought. "He and Master Z are friends, and he's been a club member for years. He used to come with his wife, but she died, and he hasn't been seriously involved with anyone since. Z said he's changed; apparently, he used to laugh a lot more. He helps with the beginners, and you certainly aren't the first new sub he's taken under command. Oh, and the subs say he's one of the best Doms in the place."

Kari breathed out. Was she pleased or unhappy with this information? Knowing he was a respectable Dom—and didn't *that* sound like a contradiction in terms—meant she had no excuse to back out. And she both wanted to and didn't want to stop before anything got more intense. She sighed and finished her drink.

"It's scary stuff when you're not used to it." Jessica pursed her lips and gave Kari a wry look. "And even when you *are* used to it. If you have a good Dom, that sense of uneasiness can be pretty exciting."

Kari glanced toward the front and saw the group of dungeon monitors reentering the room. Master Dan's gaze scanned the room. When his eyes came to rest on her, the floor seemed to drop a few inches, leaving her dizzy. Apparently, his look was even more potent than the other Doms.

He strode over to the bar, his gait long and powerful, and

stood so close she could feel the heat radiate off his body. He smiled at Jessica. "Thank you for staying with her," he said. "Kari, did she answer your questions?"

Kari nodded.

His hand tilted her chin up so he could look directly in her eyes. "Do I have your trust? Do you want to continue?"

She bit back the yes that wanted to escape from her lips. *Think, Kari.* But she knew the answer, and it wasn't changing. "*He's one of the best,*" Jessica said. That must be better than blundering around with beginners. "Yes," she said. "Continue." Oh God, was she insane?

She glanced at Jessica, and her uncertainty must have shown.

Jessica gave her a sympathetic look. "I'll get back to Z then." She shook her finger at Master Dan. "You be nice to her."

Master Dan frowned. "If you were mine, I'd beat you more often."

Appalled, Kari sucked in a breath and then saw a smile pull at his lips, the gleam of laughter in his eyes.

And Jessica only laughed as she slid off the stool and moved away.

Grasping Kari around the waist with hard hands, Master Dan lifted her off the stool and set her on her feet. Startled, she clung to his arms for a second, getting her balance. "All right, Kari. From our discussion earlier, I plan to touch you with my hands wherever I want and use light restraints. No gags, blindfolds, or impact toys—although I might spank you if you annoy me. Do you have a problem with any of that?"

Breathe, dummy. She shook her head no.

"Then here are the rules for the rest of the evening. You do what I say. Immediately. Without arguing. You don't speak unless I ask you a question. If you say anything, it had better be 'yes, Sir.' You will address me as either Sir or Master Dan."

His voice roughened. "What do you say to me, little sub?"

Startled, she jerked, then bit her lip before answering slowly, "Yes, Sir."

"Very nice. Now let's see if I remember where we were before the lessons started." He pulled her closer. And closer until she was plastered against his body, her breasts flattened on his wide chest. He bent, taking her mouth gently, tipping her back until she grabbed his shoulders for balance. He held her easily while he plundered her lips, his tongue plunging into her mouth until her head swam. When he pulled back, her hands were buried in his hair. With a laugh, he set a hand on her bottom to press her against a hard erection. "This is what that soft, hot mouth of yours does to me," he whispered in her ear.

Her insides flared with heat.

Clamping an arm around her waist, he led her to the back of the room. They passed roped-off areas along the wall, each with a different piece of ominous-looking equipment: benches, something that looked like a sawhorse with a shelf on each side, a massive wooden X against the wall. Some had shackles and cuffs, and Kari's eyes widened as she tried to imagine how a person would be attached.

Master Dan smiled slowly. "Next time, you will see more of the equipment. And use some of it."

Oh...my. She imagined herself cuffed to the bench or on that thing against the wall, and her lower regions actually tingled. "Um. Where are we going?"

They went past a small island of plants, and he turned into a sitting area with a couch and chairs. A coffee table had the requested RESERVED sign on it. "Right here. This is as private as we're going to get tonight." He pulled her down onto the couch beside him and gripped her shoulders. "All right, Kari. What's your safe word?" he asked.

Kari looked up at him. His face was serious, the humor gone. And she was alone with him.

CHAPTER FIVE

Dan smiled as she looked at him with wide eyes. She had no idea how those helpless looks could affect a Dom.

"Red," she whispered. She bit her lip again, and he couldn't stand it.

"If anyone nibbles those lips, it will be me," he murmured, licking over the plump bottom one. He tilted his head and took her mouth, then delved deep inside. She tasted of rum and Coke and something that was essentially Kari.

She sighed, her muscles softening as need overcame her fears.

She was a challenge, and he hadn't enjoyed anyone so much in ages. He could see the passion in her, locked deep inside all those habits and rules. Even more, he could see she was sweet down to the bone, much like Marion had been. But different. Marion had enjoyed her passions; this little sub had definitely been raised by nuns.

Enfolding her in his arms, he pressed her back onto the couch. Her arms wrapped around his neck, pulling his lips back to hers. He nuzzled her neck, enjoying the light fragrance—softly floral with a woman's subtle musk beneath. He wanted to explore further, to find all the places on her body where her scent was strongest.

He would get there, step-by-step.

As he deepened the kiss, she gave him anything he asked for, sucking his tongue into her mouth, giving him hers in return.

When he drew back to lean on his elbow, she made a little sound of disappointment. He studied her for a moment. A pulse beat fast in her neck; her lips were appealingly swollen and red, and her eyes heavy lidded with passion.

She was ready for more. Keeping his gaze on her, he set his hand under her long dress, slowly stroking up and down her leg, ever more upward, until he could set his palm on her crotch. She jumped a little, but he didn't move. He could feel the warmth from her pussy radiating outward. Her panties were damp, and he had to smother the urge to strip them off and bury himself inside her heat.

First things first. He wondered if she would ever remember the hour limit they'd started with. Nine o'clock was long past.

He caught her gaze—a little dazed, fully aroused. But if he didn't keep her off balance and moving forward, all that modesty and restraint would return. Time to let her discover the joy—and anxiety—of vulnerability. "Lower the top of your dress."

Her breath hitched, and she tried to look around, but he caught her chin and lifted his eyebrows. "What do you say to me?"

"Yes, Sir." Her delicate fingers undid the buttons down to the waist. He watched with a steady gaze as she glanced at him before sitting up and pulling her arms out of the dress.

He enjoyed the sight of her, his pleasure increasing as she flushed. So modest. Stripping would be one of the hardest tasks he could set her. But well worth it for him. She was a visual treat with her breasts almost overflowing the lacy white bra.

"You have lovely shoulders, Kari." He leaned forward so he could kiss his way across the pale white skin. She had little freckles scattered across her shoulders. He licked them and could swear they tasted like sugar. Since he was in the right place, he obligingly undid her bra. "Remove this."

She slid it from her arms and leaned forward to place it, neatly folded, on the coffee table.

There were reasons he loved women who were bigger than stick figures, and here were two of the finest reasons: abundant, lovely breasts with pale pink nipples. Under his gaze, those nipples contracted. He touched them with just his fingertips, watched them tighten even further. "When I'm through tasting these, they will be as hard as pencil erasers and a lovely dark red."

He waited for her blush, grinned, and stroked her heated cheek.

"Yes, exactly that color." He let his hand slide down—not like he was able to stop it—under one breast, savoring the heaviness. With his fingers, he swept in a circle around one breast, then the other, never touching either nipple, tormenting until she arched her chest forward for more.

"You are still overdressed, sweetheart. Remove your panties."

This time the hesitation was longer. He lifted her chin with one finger and gave her a firm look. "What do you say to me?"

"Yes, Sir," she whispered and stood. Her fingers trembled as she pulled up the dress. Her briefs were white, but low cut and lacy. Soft and innocent and sexy like Kari herself.

He knew she was no virgin, but she might as well be, given that her deeper passions had never been explored.

She pushed her panties to the floor, stepped out. The folded panties joined her bra on the coffee table. Tidy little sub.

"Good girl." He grabbed a fistful of the dress she still wore and pulled her between his knees. Trembling and soft, lush, and sweet. *Submissive.*

And all his for the moment.

. . .

Kari shook inside, feeling far too vulnerable. He was still dressed; she was half-naked. Yet every time he ordered her to do something with a voice that would accept only compliance, she got more excited. Wetter.

Now his knees pinned her in place as he gazed at her body. His eyes were so hot, so hungry, that she brought her hands up to cover her breasts.

He caught her arms, gave her a disapproving look, and pulled her hands down. "This is my body to play with this evening, little sub. Keep your hands down at your sides. In fact, put them behind your back and lace your fingers together." His rich baritone deepened. "What do you say to me?"

"Yes, Sir." She complied. Her hands behind her back made her breasts arch forward, almost right in his face.

He hummed in pleasure, leaned forward, and took one nipple into his mouth. His mouth was hot, lips firm, and as his tongue swirled around the nipple, she moaned, shocking herself.

When she tried to move back, he put an arm behind her. Fastening his grip over her laced fingers, he pulled her closer. His mouth tightened and his tongue rubbed her nipple against the roof of his mouth. Heat stabbed straight down to her core.

Then his free hand possessed her other breast, rolling the nipple between firm fingers.

"Oh, God." Her vision blurred. She needed to move, to do something. An ache of longing burst in her lower body.

His grip tightened.

"You have magnificent breasts, Kari. I'm going to enjoy them tonight." His dark brown eyes looked at her, studied her.

She looked away. This was a bar room, not a bedroom. No doors, no bed. That just wasn't right.

Even worse, she was taking a man's orders and...she liked it. Oh, she did. Each time he set those dark eyes on her, her insides softened until now her lower half felt like warm Jell-O. She didn't seem to have any control over her own body.

Releasing her, he moved to the chair. "Come and sit on my lap. You look like you need a hug," he said softly. He pulled her onto his lap and leaned her against his big chest. His heart thudded beneath her ear, slow and steady, as his arms snuggled her tighter. His hands were gentle as he stroked her back and arms until she relaxed against him, feeling like a pampered pet. She rubbed her forehead against his chest with a sigh.

"Not so bad, is it?" he murmured.

"Guess not."

"Good. Then we'll continue." Before she could respond, he tilted her back until her shoulders rested on the chair arm with her bottom on his lap.

"Hey!" She struggled to sit up, but he set a hand between her breasts.

"You stay where I put you, little sub," he growled, mouth flattening.

She froze. Her heart sped up as she got that strange, melting feeling again.

The corner of his mouth turned up. "You like being bossed around, don't you."

It wasn't a question and required no answer, thank heavens.

His eyes glinted with amusement. "We'll talk about that later. For now, you are in a very nice position." He set his hands on her breasts, stroking and massaging, teasing her nipples until they were tight and swollen and aching.

And that was before he put his mouth on her. He sucked on each nipple, rolling the peaks. He nipped one, and she gasped as a current of heat shot from her breast to her groin. Her private areas were wet, embarrassingly wet, and throbbing.

"You taste sweet," he murmured, then shook his head. "And you're making me forget my job here. Give me your wrists."

Her heart thudded hard. Setting her cuffed wrists into his broad palm was exceedingly difficult, but she managed. He reached into his pocket, pulled out a two-foot length of chain, and snapped each end to the cuffs.

"I'm being gentle with you, little sub," he said. "Your hands can be in front as long as they stay where I put them." He took her arms and pushed them over her head, making her back arch. "Do you understand?"

Why was her body almost shaking with need? "Yes, Sir."

"Very good."

He played with her breasts for a few more minutes until she had to press her lips together to keep from begging him for more.

Then he ran his fingers up under her dress. She gave him a wary look even as her core heated in anticipation of his touch. His hand felt huge, pushing her legs apart as his fingers teased her pubic hair, never quite touching her mound.

She stiffened as footsteps approached their sitting area. Three men walked around the corner. A DM and two newbies.

One was Buck. *Oh, no no no!* Her breasts bare, his hand under her skirt... What had she done? Kari made a grab for the top of her dress.

Master Dan glanced over at the men, then said to her, "Put your arms back where I placed them, sub."

He pinned her with his gaze, and she couldn't keep her arms from moving back over the arm of the chair. Her breath almost sobbed.

His gaze softened slightly. "Better." He looked at the men again and deliberately cupped her breast with his free hand. She stiffened, bit her lip to keep from moving.

Buck's hands clenched into fists, and he took a step forward. "She shouldn't—"

The DM grabbed his arm. "Buck, did I explain about interfering between a Dom and his sub?"

"Yes, but—"

"Go." The DM pushed the other two back around the plants

and paused long enough to smile. "Pretty sub, Dan. Doesn't look like she enjoys being displayed."

Master Dan shook his head. "Not this time, not with the asshole here." A grin flashed over his face. "Next time, though..."

With a snort of laughter, the DM followed after the men.

Sir's gaze returned to Kari, and he stroked her cheek. "I'm proud of you, little sub," he said, his eyes as warm now as they had been cold before. "I know you don't like being exposed like that."

The approval warmed her inside, at least until she remembered the shock on Buck's face. How the men had looked at her, and Sir had let them. "You should have covered me, or—"

His jaw hardened. "No, Kari. We discussed your interests earlier. Now that we've started, as your Dom, I decide what is correct or proper or desired. Aside from your safe word, you have no say, no opinions, no control."

Her mind seemed to split, one part going, No, that's wrong. The other half whispering, Yes, this is what I want.

He waited quietly, his fingers playing with the curls in her long hair.

Finally, she sighed.

His lips turned up. "Come to any conclusions?"

"Only that I'm confused."

"Good answer for a beginner." He kissed her, taking his time, nibbling on her lips, sucking her tongue into his mouth, giving her his. His hand circled her breast, his fingers toying with her nipples until heat spread through her again, and she arched uncontrollably.

"There we go," he murmured. "Now, I want you to stand up for me." He helped her to her feet and turned her to face him. "Sit down. Ride my legs."

As he lifted her dress, she lowered herself so she straddled his knees. The dress bunched around her legs. What was he going to do?

"Good. Now put your arms around me."

After a moment, she dropped her cuffed wrists over his head, sliding her arms down until her hands rested on his ribs. Her face was almost even with his, her breasts jutting toward his chest. When he cupped one of her breasts, she inhaled sharply at the heady feeling, the punch of increasing need. Could he tell how wet she was? The thought sat uneasily in her chest, and she tried to pull back, but the chain between her wrists was behind his back. Her heart gave a thud. Then she realized if she lifted her arms, she'd be free. Okay, she was good. She settled a little more comfortably and looked at him.

He smiled at her slowly. "Give me your right foot." He held his hand out.

She frowned. Lifting her foot that far would be really indiscreet considering she wore no panties.

"Kari," he growled, and her foot rose before she could tell it no. He grasped it in a callused hand and pushed it down between the seat cushion and the arm of the chair. "Now—" He gave her a hard look. "If that foot moves from where I put it, I'll tie it in place. Is that understood?" He waited.

The warning sent a rush of arousal through her, fully as intense as when he was touching her. "Yes, Sir."

She frowned as cool air touched her private areas. But the dress still covered her adequately. Thank goodness she'd worn a long one today.

Watching her intently, he leaned back and slid his left hand under her skirt to press against her mound.

Startled, she jumped and tried to lift her chained wrists back over his head. She couldn't. He'd trapped her chain behind his back. She tugged at her hands, and her breath sped up. She couldn't move her hands, couldn't do anything, and he had his hand between her legs. Fear shot through her, followed by a disconcerting wave of heat.

He still watched her. Now he smiled slowly and pulled his hand out from under her dress. "You like being restrained," he said softly. He showed her the wetness glistening on his fingers. "You're aroused, sweetheart."

She blushed from her breasts to her forehead, and he chuckled.

As he slid his hand back under her dress, she tugged again, feeling the world tilt at her helplessness, at the carnal feel of his fingers between her legs.

At knowing she couldn't stop him.

His free hand wrapped around the nape of her neck, pulling her forward. His mouth settled on hers, hot and demanding, and as his tongue took possession, he slid one hard finger into her. She inhaled sharply, tried to pull back, but his hand behind her head didn't release its hold.

His kiss deepened. Down below, his finger slid in and out, and she felt hot, needy, out of control. Exposed. She started to move her foot, to bring her legs together.

He lifted his head and gave her a hard look. "You don't want to do that, Kari."

She left her foot in place, her breathing heavy. His finger never stopped, and her vagina tightened around the invasion. Her raised leg trembled. And then his finger slicked out and up over her clitoris.

Her hips jerked uncontrollably. "Uhhhh." She bit down on her lip to keep from more betraying noises.

He stroked over the sensitive nub, spreading her slickness around her folds until her entire center tingled with need.

"Open more," he said and moved his legs apart, spreading her, exposing her further to his touch. "You have a soft pussy, sweetheart. And you're very tight." With his words, he slid his finger back up inside her, making her insides clench. When his thumb circled and stroked her clit, her hands curled helplessly against his sides.

With a low laugh, he pulled her forward, pushing her forehead against his hard chest. She needed the support as he stroked inside her, curling and hitting a sensitive spot, one that sent blood roaring through her veins like hot lava.

She could hear herself panting. Her hands closed into fists, unable to move from where they were pinned against his sides. She could only take what he was doing to her. His free hand stroked across her breasts, sending sharp, spiking lines of heat through her as he rolled her nipples between his fingers.

Her thighs quivered uncontrollably. Everything tightened inside her. Each stroke inside and each flick of his thumb on her clit sent her closer, until her breathing stopped and the pressure built. Waiting, waiting... He pulled his hand back and then pushed two fingers into her, the thickness stunning, and she broke as devastating pleasure burst inside her, as her vagina convulsed around his impaling fingers, as her hips bucked to his thrusts, over and over.

CHAPTER SIX

She was absolutely beautiful when she came, Dan thought. Her lips parted, cheeks flushed pink. Her chest heaved as she panted, jostling those luscious breasts. Her response was so honest.

After he'd induced the last few spasms, he removed his hand, enjoying the heady fragrance of her arousal. Releasing her wrists, he repositioned her so she could rest in his arms. He could feel her heart pounding when he cupped a breast.

Exhausted, she lay against his chest, limp as overcooked spaghetti. Damn, she was a comfortable armful. Little and round, fragrant and responsive. And sweet. He kissed the top of her head.

When her breathing slowed, she lifted her head. "Um...I... well...thank you."

He chuckled. Her cheeks were even pinker now than when she'd come. "You're welcome, little sub."

"But what about you? You didn't..." Her whispered words were muffled, her face pressed against his chest.

Sweet. "I'll survive."

"But..."

He tilted her chin up so she had to look at him. “You know, I would like nothing better than to tie you down, open you up, and bury my cock in that wet pussy.”

She inhaled sharply and quivered.

He stroked her cheek with his thumb. Silky smooth. “And you would like it too, little sub, wouldn’t you?”

Another wash of red across her face. Her pulse picked back up. She was unable to meet his eyes as she nodded.

“But you aren’t ready for that tonight, sweetie, and the time for your beginner class ends about now. I don’t think you want to have a dungeon monitor find you with your legs over my shoulders and me deep inside you.” The thought made him harden. “Right?”

Her spine straightened. She shook her head. “I think I’d better go now.”

He stroked her breasts, watched the nipples move from after-climax softness to hard points again. He hadn’t had enough time with those breasts; they weren’t nearly pink enough. But hell, it really was time to stop.

With a sigh, he grabbed her bra and helped her into it, covering the dual temptations. He buttoned her dress, nudging her hands out of the way when she tried to help. “I enjoy dressing you,” he murmured and grinned. “Of course, I enjoyed undressing you more.”

Having her entirely naked would be even better. An image of her in bed, arms chained over her head, squirming under his mouth, his fingers, his cock, made him harden even further, as if he hadn’t already been in pain since the moment his fingers touched her damp panties.

But a beginner deserved a gentle first experience, just enough to learn what being restrained felt like, but not enough to scare her.

With one hand along her jaw, he held her for his kiss, his grip tight enough that she could feel his strength and her helplessness.

Reminding her of what domination meant. When he released her, that succulent little body trembled.

"Now you have an idea of what submission means," he whispered. Was there anything headier than a woman quivering in his arms? Knowing he could take her in any way he wanted. Knowing he could make her come, over and over, by his touch.

And knowing his words alone could send her into total confusion. "Did you like being restrained, Kari?"

She wanted to shout at him. The man knew full well how embarrassed talking about sex made her, and he asked her that deliberately. Shoot, every time he held her in place, her insides went all soft and liquid, and he knew that too. Annoyance flared inside her.

"Kari. I asked you a question." His voice had that edge of command. Deeper, harder.

"Yes, dammit." He'd made her swear. She glared at him. And what kind of slutty woman was she to like being cuffed and ordered around and... Her body remembered the overwhelming feel of his fingers moving in her, on her, and she clenched inside. She wasn't going to get into a discussion about this. Absolutely not. "I liked it. Okay?"

One eyebrow raised, and his lips flattened into a hard line. He tilted her suddenly, back against his left arm, pinning her right side up against his chest. He secured her left wrist with one hand. As his arm tightened around her, his right hand slid under her skirt, between her legs, and he pushed a finger right into her.

She gasped, struggled. "What are you—"

"Be silent." He set his thumb on her still-sensitive clit, pressing firmly.

She gasped against the shock of awakening need.

"Now, I can keep you here, just like this, finger-fucking you until you're screaming for release until the entire club can hear you."

His graphic words widened her eyes with horror.

"Or you can apologize and remember how a sub addresses a Dom in this club." His finger started moving in and out, his thumb making circles on her clit, and she realized he could easily make her lose control. She pulled at her hand and got nowhere; his grip was tighter than the cuffs, and the feeling of helplessness sent arousal soaring within her.

His finger moved within her, slow and sure, then fast and hard, circles and strokes. She burned, her hips rising into his hand. He stopped suddenly, leaving her throbbing, his dark eyes on her face.

She realized she was breathing hard and pressed her lips together. Okay, so no problem. She'd cool down and—

He started again, plunging in and out, and she let out a cry, her hips thrashing uncontrollably. Oh, God, he could do just what he'd said. "I-I'm sorry, Sir. I'll be more careful. Please—"

His grin was a flash of white, then gone. "Apology accepted." When he removed his hand, her whole lower half ached with need. "And how you feel now will remind of you this lesson in the future."

She started to glare at him, got a level look, and managed to give him a tight-lipped smile.

He laughed. "Sweetheart, I hope you don't play poker."

With his hand—she could smell herself on his fingers—he turned her head and took her lips. She tried to push him away, realized her hand was still gripped in his, and again the heat rose within her. His kiss was hard, thorough, and long. It left her head spinning and her body aching even more.

When he lifted his head, she couldn't move, could only manage a shuddery breath. With a soft chuckle, he kissed her cheek and cuddled her against his big chest. She rolled her head against him, contented and a little confused.

When he held her, controlled her, she got so aroused, but when Buck did almost exactly the same things—ordering her, wanting to restrain her—she felt repelled. That didn't make any sense.

Of course, any woman with a functioning ovary would see Sir and want him. Oh, yes. But it was more than that. Part of what made her so hot and needy was the aura of power around him. No, more than that...*controlled* power.

He didn't let his body lead him around. He didn't let her lead him around either. And he was honest. She didn't have to guess if she did something right. If he wasn't happy, she found out right away. If he wanted her to do something, he said so.

And he liked her body. Liked *her*. She really liked him too. Especially right now. Getting off—when she did—always left her feeling a little lost. Vulnerable. But the way he held her so firmly against him made her feel safe. Cherished, even.

Even if she had more questions about herself than when she started, he'd given her an evening to remember.

She set her hand on his cheek, feeling the roughness of beard shadow. "Sir," she whispered and pulled his head down so she could kiss him and show him how much she appreciated his consideration.

When they broke this time, his eyes were soft as he looked down at her. "Kari," he murmured. He pulled her tighter against him, his hand stroking her shoulder. "Sweetheart, you are..."

He stopped, and his hand froze against her arm. For a moment, he looked at her as if he didn't know who she was.

"Sir?"

His brows drew together, and his arms loosened. Then he pushed her to her feet. "It's time you went home."

When he stood, she lifted a hand toward him but let it drop. "Are you mad? Did I do something wrong?"

His mouth smiled, but his eyes didn't. "No, you did nothing wrong. You're a very nice woman, Kari."

Well, talk about damned with faint praise.

Silently, he walked her back to where the DMs had herded the beginners into a group. Master Raoul appeared to check if anyone had questions and remind them the second beginners' class was Wednesday.

As the others dispersed, Kari turned to Master Dan. "Thank you for the...um, lesson." How awkward this was. She wanted to touch him, but he looked so cold.

He nodded, his face unreadable, his eyes without warmth. It was as if he'd pulled himself behind some impenetrable wall. "I'm glad you came, Kari. I hope you enjoy the next couple of lessons. Be careful with your next choice of Dom." He nodded to her and walked toward the exit.

Staring after him, she rubbed her hands over her arms, feeling a distinct chill. What had she done wrong? She had smarted off earlier, but he'd obtained his revenge for that.

She'd kissed him. Was that against the rules? Shoot, whatever she'd done, he obviously wasn't going to have anything to do with her in the future. But he could have been a little nicer about it.

She tried to work up a fit of good anger instead of feeling lost. What a jerk, walking off like that. "Fine then," she muttered to his back. "You have a nice life too." Turning, she almost ran into Sally.

The trainee had obviously overheard everything. Her gaze was full of sympathy.

"So what was that all about? Did I do something wrong?" Kari asked.

"No, girlfriend. That's just Master Dan; only he's not usually that abrupt." Sally stared after him, her brows together. "But it's not you. He never uses a sub more than one night."

"Oh." The unhappy lump in Kari's stomach grew bigger. So she was just another submissive to him. Here she'd thought there was more than that between them. God, she could be stupid about men. "Got it. Thanks, Sally."

"No problem. We subs stick together."

"Miss Kari?"

Kari turned to see the security guard. Oh, great, had she done something else wrong? "That's me."

"I'm Ben. Master Dan asked me to walk you to your car."

"I don't need an escort," she said, then hesitated. Buck lingered near the room exit. "Then again, I'd love the company. Thank you."

As they walked past Buck, he gave her a sheepish smile. "Kari, I wanted to apologize. I was nervous and took it out on you." He glanced at the guard. "I don't want to keep you from leaving. How about I call you later this week and we'll talk? I hope you can forgive me."

What could she say? After the way Master Dan had brushed her off like a nasty bug that had landed on his arm, Buck's eagerness to be with her was comforting. She moved her shoulders and gave him a weak smile. "There's really nothing to forgive. We'll talk later this week."

"Great." He nodded at Ben and strode away, his step with a bounce in it.

Well, at least one person thought she was nice. A shame Master Dan didn't feel the same.

Dan stalked into his apartment, stripping off his leathers on the way to the bedroom. He threw them into the corner. *What a crappy evening.*

In the kitchen, he grabbed a beer and sucked half of it down before dropping into his chair in the living room. The cold brew helped, but he was still pissed, and he thumped his head against the back of the chair. What the hell was wrong with him, anyway?

Like he didn't know. He saw her again, like he'd been seeing her every few minutes on the drive home: Kari soft and round in his arms, her eyes glazed with passion, her lips swollen from his mouth. He hardened further if that could be possible. Hell, he'd been hard all night.

He should have grabbed Sally or one of the other trainees and obtained some relief before leaving. So why the hell hadn't he? Because Kari would have felt betrayed? He wasn't married to her, involved with her; why should her feelings matter?

And there... That was the problem, the reason he felt like shit right now. The little sub had gotten to him. She didn't look like Marion, and her personality was very different, but she sure as hell brought out his possessive nature. *She's mine, her body is mine, that laugh is mine. That swollen mouth is mine, and I made it look like that.*

But she wasn't Marion. No one could be.

He opened his eyes, his gaze falling to the photograph sitting on an end table. Marion on a spanking bench, leaning so far forward her lovely breasts spilled out of the black corset. Laughter filled her face as she dared him to take her.

She was dead. All that life, that passion gone.

His fault, dammit. After being called back to the station that night, he'd canceled the evening they'd planned. She'd yelled at him and then gone out to party without him. It had been raining...

Too much alcohol, too fast, too wet.

The highway patrol had called him at the station that night. He hadn't believed them. Fuck, he hadn't accepted her death for a good year after.

If he'd stayed home, she wouldn't have died. He knew that. Even though his grief had finally eased, the guilt had become part of him. Sometimes he felt as if he'd already joined her, become just another cold, gray body in the morgue.

He studied the photo. She'd loved him, truly loved him; he'd always known that. But she would have moved on by now.

He couldn't. And so, no matter how that little sub made him feel, he wouldn't see her again.

Tipping his head back, he finished the beer. Considering how rude he'd been when he left her, she'd undoubtedly gotten the message that she was on her own. Why didn't that make him feel better?

Dressed in her robe and pajamas, Kari picked up the cup of herbal tea and took it out to her small backyard patio. The wide swing rocked gently as she curled up and leaned her head back on the cushions. What a very strange night.

The phone had been ringing as she walked in the door. Buck, calling to check that she got home safely. He'd apologized again before hanging up. She frowned. Sometime in the next day or so, she'd have to decide if she wanted to see him again. Her first few dates with him had been fun, so maybe she was being oversensitive about his behavior at the club. He'd probably been nervous, and some people became hypercritical when stressed.

Then again, he hadn't been stressed last week. She giggled, remembering how he'd instructed her on the proper way to fold hand towels. Talk about nitpicky. Perhaps this would be a good time to call it quits.

She took a sip of tea. The chamomile scent drifted up from the cup and mingled with the fragrance of her roses. Her tiny tiered fountain gurgled pleasantly, the water glinting in the moonlight. A breeze rustled through the bushes and flowers, lifting the muggy heat.

As she rocked the swing, the soft pajamas chafed her breasts, her nipples so tender the thin cotton fabric felt like sandpaper. Her thoughts drifted back to the club. How could she ever process all her impressions?

That BDSM stuff had put her into a constant state of arousal, and everything Master Dan had done only increased it. From holding her arms down and kissing her, to the helplessness of having her hands cuffed together, to being pinned in the chair with his fingers—his *fingers*—inside her. That memory made her entire private area ache and dampen.

He'd called that area her *pussy*. Since starting to teach high school, she'd heard the oddly descriptive term a time or two, but it certainly never appeared in any biology textbook.

She set the swing to rocking again. Although his fingers, his mouth—heck, everything he'd done—had been stimulating, the huge difference had come from feeling helpless, from having no control.

She'd never been so excited in her life. Had never had an orgasm like that...ever. And God, she wanted to do it all over again.

But she wouldn't have Master Dan with her next time. The thought made her stomach twist, so she sipped more tea. He had been...overwhelming. She couldn't get him out of her mind, how his face had looked when he'd touched her. The way he'd watched her so intently. How he'd pushed her, controlled her.

Jessica said there were other experienced Doms. Would she feel the same with one of them? Would they have the same deep laugh, firm hands...? She sighed, remembering the hard, clean line of his jaw, the corded muscles in his neck. Would they have those?

No, probably not. But she'd discovered something about herself tonight. The way her body reacted to domination was what she'd been looking for all her life. Master Dan's control had filled a need inside her. Scary as the thought of returning to the club alone might be, she wasn't going to stop now.

CHAPTER SEVEN

The warm tropical breeze lifted Kari's hair as she hurried up to the Shadowlands on Wednesday evening. She scowled at the setting sun. She was late. The stupid car had overheated, forcing her to drive slower. She really needed to get it to the repair shop.

She'd always hated being tardy, but it was far, far worse tonight. Her stomach churned as if she'd eaten worms for lunch instead of her usual tuna sandwich. And she probably should have eaten supper instead of changing clothes fifteen times; she still had not found anything appropriate.

What if everyone was here already? This was just so not like her, going someplace alone. At least Buck had accompanied her on Monday, even if that hadn't lasted long. She grinned briefly.

Her smile faded as she remembered who had taken his place. And how unhappily the evening had ended.

But if she didn't attend this class, she'd feel like a coward, like Master Dan had driven her away. She wiped her damp hands on her dress and raised her chin. To heck with Sir anyway; she'd darned well have fun with someone else.

The tall oak doors were open. Sucking in a breath, she walked inside. Behind the desk, the big guard rose, and a smile lightened his battered face. "Welcome back, Miss Kari."

"Thank you, Ben."

He flipped through the file box on the desk, found her name, made a check on the card. "Give me your shoes and socks; then you can go right in." He pointed to the door on the far wall, not the one that led to Master Z's office. Apparently, she didn't have to go through the screening process again.

After setting her blue-striped sneakers and pink socks on his desk, she looked at the door and hesitated. Last chance to escape. Her feet didn't want to move. After a minute, she glanced at the guard.

His brows drew together, making him look just plain mean. "Did you have trouble here last time?" he growled. "Something I should know about?"

Oh heavens. "No, not at all. Everyone was very nice." Did putting cuffs on a woman fall into the nice category? "I'm just..." She sighed and confessed, "I'm working up my nerve. I'm not used to going places like this by myself, you know?"

"Gotcha." Ben grinned at her. "You don't have the look of a loner. Hang on just a sec." He pressed a button on his desk.

"No, wait!" *Too late.*

"What?" The bartender's voice barked out of the intercom.

"If Jessie's in there, can you ask if she'd escort one of the newbie subs inside? She's feelin' a little lonely."

A snort. "If she's a sub, she won't be lonely long." A pause. "She's on her way out."

Kari felt like a kindergartner refusing to walk into school on the first day. "I would have—"

"Nah." Ben sat back down at the desk. "Don't worry. You're not the first novice to get scared, won't be the last."

The inner door opened, and the woman whom Kari had met on Monday trotted out, her blonde hair bouncing. "Hey, I was hoping you'd be back."

Kari smiled, pleasure mingling with relief. "Thanks for rescuing me. I'm not sure why I froze."

"Been there, done that." Jessica grinned at the guard. "Right, Ben?"

He shook his head. "You were trouble from the beginning. Get a move on. I think she's the last to arrive."

"In that case, let's get you in before Raoul gets all huffy." Jessica pushed Kari through the doors and into the club room.

Trying not to be obvious, Kari looked around for Master Dan. His tall figure didn't appear, and disappointment grew inside her, making her chest ache.

As they passed the bar, the bartender, Master Cullen, grinned at Kari. "Now if I'd known it was you, I'd have gone out myself to hold your hand."

She gave him a tentative smile, unsure if he was joking or not.

At the end of the room, they found the class. Jessica patted her shoulder, whispered, "See you later," and headed away.

"Well, everyone has returned for more. I'm pleased." Master Raoul rested his hip on the back of the couch. "On Monday, we covered safe words, basic restraints, and safety issues. Now you've had a chance to practice, does anyone have questions?"

As the students shook their heads, Kari took the time to look them over. About half were obviously couples, standing beside each other, holding hands, mostly man-woman sets, with an occasional guy-guy or woman-woman. The singles divided fairly evenly between the two sexes.

"You came back." A whisper behind her and she thrilled, thinking Sir had found her. She felt his breath on her neck and glanced over her shoulder. Buck. Oh joy. He stood too close, his thighs brushing against her bottom.

"Hi, Buck." She hadn't returned his message on her answering machine. She tried to edge away without being too blatant.

"I've missed seeing you," he whispered. He ran his hand down her arm, then turned his attention to the instructor. She let out a relieved sigh.

Raoul went through the basics of domination and then coached a woman named Linda through a slave posture. Kari winced. *Slave* didn't sound as harmless as *submissive*, somehow. He explained the club dress code and about the "private play" rooms upstairs. The penalties for interrupting a scene. Cleaning the equipment.

And then he started on a tour of the room, explaining the furniture in each of the roped-off areas. He shackled one of the gay men to a big wooden X called a St. Andrew's cross. Then came a spanking bench, a bondage table, an exotic lacing table, a sawhorse, a whipping post, two cages in a corner, a spiderweb thing, a stockade. He used a different sub to demonstrate each piece of equipment.

"Kari, your turn," he called, motioning to something called a bondage chair.

She swallowed and moved forward. At least he didn't strip anyone, just demonstrated the various restraints and how each piece could be used. She seated herself on the chair. After Master Raoul fastened her ankles to the chair legs, her wrists to the chair arms, she realized the center of the seat was cut out, leaving just her buttocks perched on the edge. With legs shackled open, and the missing chair bottom, a naked person's private parts would be on display. She shivered, relieved when the instructor unfastened her.

After two more pieces of equipment, Master Raoul said, "That's it for the formal lesson. All the equipment down here is duplicated in various upstairs rooms if you prefer private play. Remember that gags are forbidden at this point in your classes. DMs will be in the hallways upstairs and down here to answer questions or intervene if there's a problem."

He looked at each sub in turn, his expression serious. "Subs, no matter what safe word you agree on with your partner, the club safe word is red. If you shout that out, a DM will come to see if everything is all right. Remember, 'safe, sane, and consensual' are the operative words here. Got that, everyone?"

People nodded.

"Remember, you discuss what you will be doing first and reach an agreement. Establish trust before you jump in. Class is dismissed. Pair up as you wish." He frowned as he counted the single newbies. "Anyone left without a partner can talk to me over at the bar."

As he walked away, the singles began talking. One couple headed out, then another. Kari saw two men watching her, one with a cruel look in his eyes that made her stomach twist, and the other would probably run if she said boo. She thought about what Master Dan had done to her, tried to imagine letting either of the men do *anything* with her, and couldn't.

"Kari, honey. How about we try using that spiderweb?" An easy smile on his face, Buck approached and set his hand on her shoulder.

Without thinking, she stepped back and shook her head. Her instinctive reaction reminded her of Master Dan asking how her body felt about something. Maybe she'd listen to her body for once. "I'm sorry, Buck. I don't want to—" *Let you have any control over me.*

That would be rude. Oh, she just wasn't comfortable saying no to people or hurting their feelings. She glanced at the diminishing group of singles and realized she didn't want to be with any of them. That solved her problem nicely. "I'm afraid I'm not staying for the practice part. But thank you for the offer."

Nolan strolled into the club room and smiled at the underlying scent of sweat, fear, pain, and sex that Z's fancy cleaning crew could never remove. Muscles he didn't know had been tight started to loosen.

As he crossed to the bar, he checked out the changes. A few new pieces of equipment—a lacing table, a spiderweb. There'd probably be a few other things in the theme rooms. Z liked toys.

"Hey, Nolan, welcome home!" Rising from a bar stool, Raoul shook Nolan's hand, a grin on his swarthy face. He glanced at Nolan's gold-trimmed vest. "I see Z already tagged you for DM duty."

"Nolan!" Cullen's yell set his ears ringing as the bartender leaned across the bar to thump his shoulder. "Damn, dude, where have you been?"

Nolan thought on it for a minute. "Here and there. Mostly Baghdad."

"No alcohol there, I bet." Cullen slid a cold Corona over.

Nolan stared at it. Nobody else drank Corona around here. "That beer over a year old?"

"Nah. Z told me you were back. I stocked up," Cullen said.

The welcome made Nolan's chest tighten. "Thanks."

"You still look like a nasty bastard," Cullen commented, ignoring a couple of newbies signaling for his attention. "You're gonna have the subs all scared and clamoring for your attention. How's your pretty slave doing, by the way?"

"I uncollared Felicia before I deployed," Nolan said. And although he'd missed her, he hadn't realized how much of a strain being a master twenty-four/seven was until she was gone. "So it's been a while. I'm looking forward to playing again." He sucked down half the brew, something else he'd missed. "Anything new?"

"Z has a sub now, a cutie. Grabbed her before she even made it through the door," Cullen said. "Hell, he had her before she even knew she was submissive, but she hooked him right back."

"Z? Hooked?" Nolan set his beer down. "Seriously?"

"Looks like. Good match," Raoul said. "I thought for a minute Dan was going to follow in his footsteps. He took on a beginner

Monday, a sweet little sub, and looked pretty involved, but he chilled out again."

"That the pretty submissive who Jessica was talking to? Kari?" Cullen asked.

"Yep." Raoul nodded toward the group of beginners. "Little, round, really polite."

"I like her." Cullen scratched his cheek. "And Dan needs someone to kick him out of his rut. When Marion died, seems like she took him with her. The asshole hardly laughs anymore." He studied the beginner class. "Yeah, she might be good for him."

"Z must have thought so. He asked Dan to take her on."

Nolan listened idly. Dan had gone through a rough time there, losing his wife like that. It was time he came out of that dark shell. Turning, he checked out the class. The singles had dwindled until only a few remained. He identified the sub whom Raoul and Cullen had mentioned, watched a wannabe Dom brace her, try for her. She not only turned the guy down but left the group entirely, heading toward the bar. Very pretty, short, and curvy like he preferred.

"Heads up," he warned Raoul. "Incoming."

Kari walked away from the other newbies, feeling like a failure. She'd made it here, attended the class, but she'd basically blown the final by not practicing what she'd learned. But she just couldn't. Not with them. Face it, she'd been hoping Master Dan would be here, would have changed his mind. *Dumb, Kari*. He'd made himself quite clear.

She started toward the door and then stopped. She should be polite and tell Master Raoul she was leaving. For all she knew, he might do a head count at the end of the night.

Master Raoul was at the bar, talking with Cullen. Beside Raoul, another DM, a big, darkly tanned man around forty, leaned on the bar, listening. With a white scar across one cheekbone and cold black eyes, the man just plain looked dangerous. She gave him a wide berth and stopped on Raoul's other side.

Cullen broke off in midsentence and smiled at her. "Little Kari, how are you?" The look he gave her warmed her right to her toes.

Ignoring the quiver in her stomach, she nodded back. "I'm fine. And how are you?" *Oops*. "Ah...Sir."

Cullen and Raoul chuckled. The other man didn't even smile.

"Very nice," Cullen said. "Can I get you something to drink, or is someone waiting for you?"

"No, thank you." She turned to Master Raoul. "I'm going to call it an early night, but I enjoyed your class very much. Thank you." She nodded and moved toward the door.

"Stop." Master Raoul's command had a snap in it.

Kari's feet froze before her brain had processed the word. She turned.

"Are you having a problem with one of the other beginners?" Master Raoul's eyes narrowed as he inspected the class.

"No, not at all. I just am not—" She couldn't think of a way to say this politely. "I feel uncomfortable with—" *With beginners*. She shrugged rather than finish. "I see no need to practice, so I'll head out. I appreciate your concern."

He'd been studying her face. "Going from Master Dan to a beginner... I see the problem. I'll find you an experienced Dom."

"No, really, I'm—"

"You know, I've had a little experience," Master Cullen said mildly.

Raoul snorted. "Like fifteen years or so?"

"About that." Cullen lifted his head and shouted toward the front of the room, "Dan! Man the bar. I'm taking some playtime." He ducked under the bar and towered over Kari. "I'll top you tonight."

She managed to close her mouth. "Well..." Experienced, for sure. More easygoing than Sir—or at least more talkative. The set of his jaw, the way he watched her expressions made her think he might be as intimidating as Sir.

There wasn't the same sense of connection with him or the trust she'd felt with Master Dan. But so what. Her reasons for being here were still valid. "Thank you. I'd like that."

Kari heard footsteps behind her, then Master Dan's voice with a hint of laughter. "You and your damned playtimes. I'll babysit the bar for a couple of hours, but that's it, Cullen."

Sir's deep, rough voice singed through every pathway in Kari's body, and her insides melted like a sun-warmed chocolate bar. She stiffened but didn't turn around. Cowardly, but she didn't want to see his face turn cold again.

Cullen looked down at her, and a smile flickered over his hard-hewn face. He put a heavy arm across her shoulders and mashed her against his side. And then, hand gripping her shoulder so she couldn't escape, he turned them both to face Master Dan.

"Well, Dan, I'm not sure I'm going to want to stop at two hours." Cullen rubbed his knuckles gently across her cheek. "Little Kari looks like she's got more stamina than that."

Master Dan saw her, and his face turned to stone. Even as his gaze dissected her like a bug, his mouth thinned. His anger hit her like a fist to the chest.

Kari pulled in a shaky breath and tried to back away, despite the restraining arm around her shoulders. What had she done to make him so mad at her?

"Dan, buddy, you got a problem?" Cullen asked, his voice as easy as if Sir didn't look murderous. Raoul's eyes narrowed.

Sir's gaze never left Kari as his jaw tightened. He inhaled slowly as his iron will imposed control. When his eyes released Kari, she almost staggered.

Sir's gaze rested on the bartender and then a corner of his mouth curved upward. "You asshole. Your fucking sense of humor is going to get you killed one of these days. Maybe today."

Kari wrapped her arms around herself. She'd seen quite a bit of fighting in the schools, but these two guys were huge. They'd destroy the whole bar.

"I haven't enjoyed anything so much in days." Cullen's laugh boomed in the quiet room. "But you know, you're scaring *my* sub." His hand squeezed her shoulder, pulled her a little closer.

CHAPTER EIGHT

Dan's hands fisted as possessiveness burned through him in a red-tinged wave. One more word and he'd knock his fucking friend across the room. "Don't push me."

Cullen grinned.

Dan moved closer. When Kari's big blue eyes lifted to meet his, his breath was sucked away. He couldn't keep from touching her long, wavy hair, running his fingers down her soft cheek. She trembled. He'd scared her, dammit.

Cullen cleared his throat. "Dan, I think—"

Dan kept his eyes on Kari. "Go away, Cullen. Playtime's over. She's mine." He sucked in a breath and corrected himself. "Mine for this evening."

"I should make you work a little harder, but okay." Cullen dropped his arm. "Kari, I'll be here if you need me." He moved away.

Dan held out his hand. How badly had he damaged her trust? She couldn't possibly understand his behavior, considering he didn't understand it himself. "Let's talk."

Her eyes wary, she chewed on her lip, and he hardened at the memory of how soft those lips had been. She shook her head, and his mouth tightened. He'd never forgive himself for—

"I must be crazy," she muttered and set her hand in his.

The relief almost swamped him. He led her to a nearby couch and pulled her down beside him. She wore another long dress, but this one was silky and a true blue color that matched her eyes. The top dipped low enough to display the beginning curve of her breasts, and with her full figure, it was provocative as hell.

His plans had definitely changed for the night, from wanting to avoid her to wanting to strip her naked. If he could talk her into it.

Having regained her composure, she tapped a finger on his arm. "I got the impression that you were a one-night stand sort of guy."

"I am." He laid his hand over her delicate fingers, realized her hands were chilled, and clasped them in his. "To be honest, Kari, I don't get involved with anyone. I've found that if I keep encounters to one night, there're no hurt feelings."

"Then why did you take me from—" She glanced toward the bar and Cullen.

A flare of jealousy bit into his stomach like acid for the second time in five minutes. *Dammit.* "I'm here; you're here," he said, keeping his tone light.

He paused. Honesty was essential between a Dom and sub; if he wasn't willing to bare his thoughts, how could he demand the same from her?

"No, it's more than that," he said. He pulled her closer, slid an arm behind her back. "I don't know what's going on between you and me, but it's not finished yet." He looked away from her, and Marion's face rose in his mind, more shadowy than normal. "When I lost my wife, I lost everything. I don't have anything to give. Only sex for a night." He didn't have more. He didn't *deserve* more. "So I can't offer you a commitment other than I want you tonight."

"That's no commitment at all." She stared across the room, her gaze on someone using the bondage table. After a minute, she shook her head like a dog shedding water. "But it's enough. That's all I want too. Just sex."

"Well, that I can give."

"I know," she said under her breath, then looked at him with a smile. "I was looking forward to exploring more of this BDSM stuff, but the other beginners..." She frowned, obviously searching for the right words. "It seemed too much like the blind leading the blind."

"Now that *would* be frightening." He took her chin, looked into her eyes. "Are you afraid of me?"

She tilted her head. "Not...exactly. I trust you, but I'm a bit scared of what you might do."

"Well, little sub, that *is* the point. Do you remember your safe word?"

"Red."

"Good." He unclipped something from a metal ring on his left side. "I almost forgot your jewelry. Give me your wrists."

She hesitated, then laid her wrists into his hand.

He buckled on fleece-lined leather cuffs. "What the well-dressed sub wears in the Shadowlands. Master Z would have been displeased if he'd seen your wrists naked."

As she frowned at them, he pulled her onto his lap, his arms holding her against his big chest. She felt just right. "Now, let's run through what might happen here tonight."

"Okay." Dropping her cuffed wrists to her lap, Kari leaned her head against his shoulder. Cullen probably would have been nice, but he wasn't Master Dan. She really did trust Sir to keep her safe. His solid arms felt good—just right—around her.

At least until his fingers pulled down the zipper on the front of her dress. His hand slid under her bra and closed over her left breast.

"Wait." She tried to pull away, but his other hand gripped her hip, holding her in place. God, she'd forgotten how strong he was, how big. Her insides quivered as her breathing increased.

"The restrictions for a beginner's first night are gone, Kari," he murmured, his thumb stroking her nipple to a hard peak, the controlled power of his grip making her shake. "Unless you object now, tonight, I can—and I will—take you, with my hands. My mouth. My cock. Any way I want. As many times as I want."

With his hand on her breast, he could undoubtedly feel her breathing increase, her pulse speed up. "Your body likes that idea," he whispered. "I intend to play with you, to restrain you, maybe even to show you off. I might spank you. Tell me now if that's a problem."

She wanted it all—and it all terrified her. What was she thinking to allow this?

His gaze was on her face. When she didn't tell him no, he continued, "All right then. Your safe word is still red—use it if you need to. Otherwise, your only response to anything I want will be, 'yes, Sir.'"

Need clawed into her as her insides turned liquid. She dampened.

As if he could tell—and he probably could, the jerk—he whispered, "Are you wet for me now, little sub?"

Her body didn't feel like her own anymore. Yes, she'd wanted to explore sex here, but this was too fast. Too much.

When she didn't answer, he removed his hand from her hip and tilted her head to meet his gaze. His eyes crinkled as he studied her face. "You're flushed. Your pulse is hammering. Your breathing is fast. Kari, either answer my question, or I will check for myself. Right here."

She gasped and closed her legs tightly at the thought of his hand under her skirt, right in the center of the room. This wasn't at all like that isolated spot he'd found for them last time. Didn't he understand anything about privacy? Discretion? Politeness? She pushed at his hand and gritted out, "Fine. I'm wet. Okay?"

The minute the words left her mouth, she remembered his response the last time she'd snapped at him, and her world tipped sideways.

His eyes went cold. "No, that answer is as far from okay as it can get. Open your legs for me now."

"I will not." She tried to move from his lap, and his grip tightened.

"Since you like multiple choice, here you go. *A:* You can be an example for the other subs when I drag you to the bondage table, strap you down, and let everyone see how wet you are."

Her breath choked in her throat as horror filled her.

"Or *B:* You may apologize for your tone, and I'll let you open your legs for me here." He gave her a hard look, and she knew he'd do just what he said. "Which is it, little sub?"

"Here," she whispered. "I'm sorry, Sir. Please stay here."

He pulled her dress up to her knees, set a hand on her bare leg, and waited.

She tried to look around, to see if anyone could see her.

"Do it now, sub, and keep your eyes on me," he ordered in a glacial voice. His command sent disconcerting heat washing through her.

Biting her lips, she eased her legs apart. His right hand stroked up between her thighs, forcing her to open farther until his palm pressed against her mound. She glanced down and turned red. Her dress was pushed up, barely covering her, and anyone could see the location of his hand.

People walked past the couch. A woman in a black bustier, fishnet stockings, and high heels glanced over and grinned. Over by the spanking bench, Buck stared at Sir, his mouth twisting into an ugly line. Then there were Master Raoul and Master Cullen at the bar...

With a low moan, Kari shoved at her skirt.

Master Dan sighed, lifted his left hand from her hip. "Give me that hand."

Darn it, she knew what he planned—one arm pinned against his chest, the other in his grip. She'd have no choice but to let him do what he wanted.

He chuckled. "And that just made you wetter." Oh, God, he had his fingers pressed into her crotch.

"Hand, Kari."

Giving up, she set her hand in his. He closed his fingers around her wrist and set both their hands against her hip, holding her wedged in one place. She had a moment to feel her helplessness, and then he slid under the edge of her panties and pushed a finger inside her. Her hips jerked at the suddenness of the entry, at the flaring arousal that soared through her.

"Yes, you're very wet." His finger moved inside her, sent jolts of sensation through her. "Makes me want to bend you over the couch and bury myself in you."

He could undoubtedly feel the way her vagina clamped down as well as she could. Oh, God.

"But I think we'll go upstairs so I can take my time exploring your body." His eyes crinkled. "You like that idea too, don't you? Answer me, sub."

"Yes, Sir." His finger moved, stroked the walls of her vagina in erotic circles.

"Afterwards, I'll bring you back down here." He glanced at the St. Andrew's cross. "I could strip you and bind you up there."

She stiffened, the thought exciting. Appalling.

"Ah, not quite ready for that yet, are you?" He nibbled on her ear. "Even if I left your clothes on, I could put you in the stockade, lift your skirt, and take you there."

His finger moved within her. "Not that yet, either, although the interest is there, isn't it?"

She had no answer for him, confusion and fear and arousal so mingled inside her that she couldn't think at all. The way he had her restrained with just his body, his hands, made her feel so strange. So needy. She looked at him, unable to speak.

His smile was hard, satisfied. "I like that look on your face." He bent his head and took her lips ruthlessly, satisfying himself. His finger thrust in and out of her below, the twin assaults swamping her mind in desire. She trembled as urgent need coursed through her.

When he pulled away, his eyes were heavy lidded with passion, dark with promise. "Let's go, sub. I have things I want to do to you."

He gave a low laugh, and she knew he'd felt the clench of her insides around his finger.

He removed his finger, making her jerk, leaving her throbbing. Pushing her to her feet, he wrapped a hard arm around her waist. "If you talk fast, I'll let you choose the room."

He kept her hand firmly in his as he led her up the spiral stairs in the front corner of the room. At the top, at the sight of doors running down a long hallway, she pulled back. *Sex*. She was going to have *sex* this time. This was—

"Little sub, you worry so much your head must ache." He pulled her into his arms, and his embrace turned comforting. Warm. "You're aroused. And scared." He nibbled on her neck, then kissed her until her knees sagged and the world spun.

Pulling back, he looked at her. "Blue is definitely your color. Let's go with that."

Halfway down the hall, he opened a door to a small room. Candles in sconces on the gray-blue walls provided a soft, flickering light. Classical music came from speakers somewhere in the room. The room had a bed with a dark red velvet cover and a big armoire. Velvet ropes dangled from the headboard; more ropes with leather cuffs were tied to the foot of the bed. A chill crept up Kari's spine, followed by excitement. Would he really use those on her?

Placing his hands on her shoulders, he steered her to stand beside the bed. Running a hand down her front, he chuckled, realizing she'd raised the zipper. With a firm hand, he pulled it all the way down. As her dress gaped open and the air hit her overheated skin, she shivered and her nipples peaked, showing through her thin lacy bra.

He touched one breast, stroking over the hard bud. His gentle finger sent little ripples of need through her.

After a second, he nudged her dress off, letting it pool at her feet, leaving her in her white bra and panties.

"Your underwear is very much like you," he said. "The white for sweet, sheer lace for sexy." One hard hand held her upper arm as he ran a finger across the top of her bra, his finger warm, slightly abrasive, the touch sensitizing her skin. There was something erotic about being forced to stand still, not being able to move as a man played with her body, pleasing himself.

"Remove your bra, Kari," he said, stepping back and watching her with narrowed eyes.

She fumbled with the catch, embarrassed, yet wanting his hands on her so badly her mouth was dry. The flickering lights weren't bright, but she still felt awfully exposed as her breasts spilled free. He cupped his hands under them, squeezing slightly, enough to make her suck in a breath. Enough for heat to flow through her. "Now the panties can go."

Feeling awkward, she pushed them off and let them slide to the floor. His eyes on her felt hot. He smiled slowly. "You're a lovely woman, Kari. I'm going to enjoy taking you."

The blunt words, so openly carnal, thrilled her. Confused her.

Gripping her upper arms, he raised her onto her toes and took her lips in a hot, wet kiss, exploring her mouth until her hands fisted with the need to touch him. He drew back and traced her swollen lips with his finger.

"Up on the bed with you." He patted behind him.

Oh, God, she really *was* going to do this.

As she crawled up onto the bed and turned to sit, he tossed his vest on the ground, opened his leathers. Oh heavens, he was even more muscled than she'd realized, and he was...huge, his erection past his belly button. Thick and hard and... "I don't—um—You're awfully big," she ventured.

He grinned as he sheathed himself in a condom. "We'll fit, sweetie." Joining her on the bed, he pressed her down onto her back and covered her with his body, his heat unbelievable. She ran her hands over his shoulders, amazed at the contoured muscles of his back, how they tightened to rock hard with each movement.

He bit her neck, licked the spot, bit again, the pain sharp and erotic.

"Open your legs for me."

She hesitated despite the arousal urging her on. He was so big...

He chuckled. "Don't worry, by the time I enter that sweet pussy, you'll be begging me." He kissed her hard, forcefully. "Open your legs, Kari."

She parted her legs, and he slid between them. She could feel his penis against her entrance, the feeling exciting. Making her shiver.

"You know, I wasn't planning to do this until later, but I tire of repeating each command," he murmured, and he kissed her again, taking her mouth deeply. When he pulled back, she realized her right arm was fastened above her head, a thick rope securing her cuff to the headboard.

"Hey!"

He lifted her other arm and secured the wrist cuff to a rope before she'd gotten past the surprise of the first.

"Wait. I don't—"

One knee on each side of her hips, he sat up. His balls bumped against her pussy, making her jump. As his weight on her legs pinned her to the bed, she pulled on the ropes; her breathing increased. She was tied to the bed. *Tied*. Before, she could at least move; now her cuffs were fastened to something. She couldn't even run.

He tilted his head, studied her as she pulled at the ropes. Leaning forward, he held her face between his two hands, his eyes a rich brown. She stilled, feeling like a trapped animal, a shivering mouse held in someone's grip.

His rough voice was quiet. "Are you in pain, Kari?"

"No, but..."

"No, what?"

He wasn't serious, was he? She was tied up, and he was sitting on her. And yet, she was horrified to feel herself getting wetter and wetter.

His hands left her face to stroke her breasts, circling the sensitive nipples until she pressed up for his touch. "No, what?"

His hands lifted, waited.

She was breathing hard and her answer huffed between her lips. "No, Sir."

"Very good." His fingers closed on her nipples, pulling, rolling, each movement just one tiny step short of real pain, each squeeze sending zings of sensation straight to her groin. "Such sensitive breasts." He bent to suck one nipple into his mouth, working it, the feeling so intensely pleasurable, she cried out. He switched to the other.

"Look, Kari," he said, his fingers pulling gently. "See how beautiful."

Her breasts were swollen, tight with the nipples darkened to deep rose and spiking upward like tiny pencils. "Say, 'My breasts are beautiful.'"

"My breasts are beautiful." And they were too.

His eyes warmed with approval before he slid down her body, pressing kisses to the undersides of her breasts, nuzzling her stomach. He nipped next to her belly button, making her squeak with surprise. And then he was *there*. Just looking at her most private of places. Her pussy.

Totally embarrassed, she tried to close her legs.

He pushed back to lean on his heels and narrowed a stern gaze at her. "My body to play with," he repeated. "Open your legs for me."

She slid them out, feeling the flush working its way up her chest. She was so wet, he'd see, know she was—

"Farther." And he just sat there, waiting. In charge. *Dominant*.

She slid her legs farther apart, feeling her...her *everything* open. Totally exposed.

"Very nice. You have a lovely pussy, no matter how you try to conceal it. And I'm going to enjoy it in so many ways." He pressed his hand to her there, right between her legs. "I'm going to lick it all over."

She could feel herself dampen and so could he. "Maybe I'll use a vibrator, pushing it deep inside you." Her vagina actually clenched, and he grinned wickedly, his eyes crinkling. He felt every little involuntary movement she made.

He positioned himself between her legs, his shoulders between her knees. She could feel his breath on her inner thighs, and her legs started to close against the intimacy.

"Keep them open, Kari, or I will tie them open." And they both felt her wetness increase.

"You are a surprising woman, little sub." He chuckled as he rolled off the bed, one ankle already in his hand. Grabbing the fleece-lined cuff roped to the footboard, he buckled it on and tightened the rope, imprisoning her leg at an angle. He snatched her other ankle as she was trying to decide if she should fight, and there she was, spread-eagled. Just like her fantasies, only this was real. Maybe too real.

The instinctive need to be free had her pulling at the ropes holding her wrists. Her chest squeezed with fear as she tried to kick her legs, and the restraints held. He stood at the foot of the bed and watched silently. Waited until she stopped.

He lay down between her legs. With her legs pulled outward, everything was open for him.

"You have a pretty, pretty pussy, Kari. Hidden within those little brown curls"—he pulled her pubic hair lightly, tantalizingly —"everything is pink." One finger slowly slid down the outer labia. "You're very wet for me, can you tell?" He touched her right over the entrance, swirled a finger inside just long enough to make her squirm with pleasure.

When he took his fingers away, leaving her aching, she whined like a child.

"We have time, sweetheart, and I'm going to take my time."

She almost blurted out a protest. *Take me now; put your hands on me now*. She managed to close her lips.

He stroked down her thigh, his hand so big that his fingers could curl underneath. His knuckles traced the path back up, across her tender, sensitive inner thigh, lightly over her pubis, and down the other leg. Almost to the right spot. Exquisite torture. Her fingernails dug into her palms as he stroked her legs, the curls on her pubis, the soft crease where her hip met her leg.

Her clitoris throbbed more with each pass, with each time he didn't touch her where she so needed to be touched. "Please," she whispered, aching with longing.

"What do you call me?" he asked, touching her with just one finger, so close, edging so close.

She arched up. "Please, Sir, please."

"Nicely said, sweetheart," he murmured approval. And he slid the finger right into her.

"Aaah." The nerves inside her vagina flared to life with the intimate invasion.

He lowered his mouth to her clit, a touch like butterfly wings. She arched again, tightening around his finger, needing more than the light flicks on her clit. She was so close. The world narrowed to just the feel of his hands, his mouth. One more touch...

He pulled his finger out, emptying her, and lifted his head.

Nooo. She whimpered a protest.

"You don't have permission to come."

"What?" she whispered shakily.

"You come when I say, not before."

"You can't—"

"Kari," he warned in a hard voice. "I've been patient, but my patience is at an end. Did you get taught about punishment in your class?"

Not really. But the way he'd sent Sally off to be punished... She didn't want anything like that to happen to her. Her thighs shook with her need. "Sir, I'm sorry."

"Very nice." He lowered his head, licked up her labia, sucking one into his mouth, then the other, the sensation like hot velvet. His tongue laved right there in the center. *Oh God, almost*. Not far enough, she needed more.

Then one finger opened her, sliding in ever so slowly and back out. She tightened around him, her legs quivering uncontrollably. In again, his finger large, pressing down to add friction, out.

Two fingers. She moaned at the added sensation as his fingers drove into her, faster, harder. Her whole pussy was afire, wanton hunger burning through her. She strained against the restraints as his mouth came down on her. His tongue slid over her clitoris and around it, swirling and rubbing as his fingers plunged in and out.

She panted, her bottom pushing off the bed, closer, closer. "Ah, ah—"

And he stopped, took his hands away. "Not yet."

"But—"

"Silence."

Her groan came from deep within her, her entire lower half too tight. Throbbing with need. She'd never felt so out of control. Never begged before. She *hurt*.

He licked the tender skin of her inner thigh, and she shuddered. His shoulders rubbed against her legs, and she trembled against the restraints.

She pulled at her wrists, wanting to touch him, to force him to touch her; she'd even touch herself if she had to. Over her head, her hands closed into fists as the feeling of helplessness roused her further, making everything worse.

He slid a finger into her again, shooting urgency through her, her arousal higher and harder than before. She moaned, her head rolling from side to side. When her hips lifted, he ruthlessly pressed her back down, holding her for his use.

He pushed his finger in, pulled out, and added another finger. Her tissues were so swollen each thrust shoved her closer and closer. His tongue flicked across her clit, and she went rigid as her muscles tightened, as her vagina clenched around his fingers. She neared the peak, held there...

"Come now, Kari," he ordered, his voice deep. Sucking her clitoris into his mouth, his tongue rubbed it hard and fast.

Her world flashed white, splintering around her, and she shattered with it. Spasms in her vagina rippled against the hard fingers impaling her, and her hips jerked uncontrollably. Her legs thrashed against the restraints, her arms pulled against the ropes, and the sensations went on and on.

When her climax started to slow, he'd move his fingers, slide his tongue across her again, and she'd arch back up as the exquisite tremors shuddered through her again. And again.

Finally, she lay limp, drenched in sweat, her heart pounding so hard her ribs must be bruised. "My God, no wonder people like being tied up," she murmured.

His hand slapped her thigh hard enough to sting.

She jumped. "Hey!"

"Did you speak, little sub?" He lifted his head, his stern eyes holding a warning.

She started to say something, thought better of it. "Sir. I'm sorry, Sir. I thought we were done. Sir."

He chuckled. Then he rose onto his knees, his big hands roved up her thighs, massaging the cramped muscles. He slid his hands up her stomach, and with a smile, cupped her breasts, squeezing just hard enough to make her breath hitch. His fingers lightly pinched her softening nipples back into attention.

"Kari, sweet, we're just getting started. In fact, I think you should come again before we move on."

No. Wait.

And he slid back down. With fingers and mouth and tongue—and teeth this time—he brought her to another orgasm. A screaming one.

Oh God, oh God, oh God. Her heart was thudding so fast it felt like a galloping horse, and her lungs labored to find enough air.

He moved back and unfastened her ankles. "Kari."

She blinked at him.

He gently pushed the sweaty strands of hair off her face and then moved on top of her, holding his weight on his elbows. "Bring your legs up," he whispered before he took her mouth, plunging his tongue in.

She could taste herself, another shock in itself. Managed—eventually—to remember what he'd said. *Legs up.* Her legs were free, and she slid them up to settle beside his hips. His penis slid in the wetness of her folds; each brush against the swollen, sensitive tissues sent tremors through her.

When his hand dropped down and pressed the head of his penis to her entrance, she moaned, shivered.

Without any more warning, he drove into her, all the way to the hilt.

"Oh!" Impaled on him, she tried to jerk away. "Oooh..." Her insides pulsed around his intrusion, and her arms futilely yanked at the restraints.

CHAPTER NINE

"Oh, sweetheart, you feel good," Dan murmured, taking her mouth again for a kiss. So good she was liable to kill him dead as her pussy squeezed his cock like a hot, pulsing fist. She was tight, slick with her own juices.

From the tightening of her muscles, the slight cringing away, he was bigger than she was used to. He got a deplorable sense of satisfaction from knowing that.

He kissed her while he waited for her body to adjust, plunging his tongue into her mouth in slow strokes, imitating what he'd be doing to her shortly. With one hand, he toyed with those sensitive nipples. The little whimpers she made could harden a dead man.

When he felt her hips start to move upward in response, he grinned and slid out—in—her moans as addictive to him as gin to an alcoholic. As he increased the speed, he released her wrists from the restraints. Her arms wrapped around him convulsively before her hands started stroking his back, adding to his pleasure.

He surged deeper, and her silken pussy contracted around him. With every hard thrust, his balls slapped against her soft buttocks, sending an inflaming vibration through him. He could feel her thigh muscles tremble as she awoke again to pleasure and moved right into true need.

What idiot could have possibly thought she was cold? Gripping her hips, he yanked her up against him with each stroke and then rubbed his pelvis down her clitoris as he withdrew. Her moans transformed into hard panting, and her fingers clenched his shoulders like miniature vises. Her little fingernails dug into his skin, arousing pinpricks of pain.

Faster, harder—she was almost there. He could feel his cock swell as he kept himself from coming. Reaching down between them, he swirled his fingers in the wetness from her pussy, then stroked up and over her clit.

She broke with a scream, spasming around him so hard his own climax engulfed him. With a roaring growl of pleasure, he buried his length within her and let her milk him dry.

Kari was still shuddering from the shock waves of pleasure when Master Dan rolled them over and nestled her to his side, her head on his chest. She could hear his heart drumming under all that muscle. His arms kept her against him, and she—she needed that right now, somehow.

He'd tied her up.

And she'd not only let him but had enjoyed everything he'd done. What was happening to her?

"You're thinking again, little sub," he murmured, kissing the top of her head. "What about?"

She'd be doing a lot of thinking, she had a feeling. Instead of answering him, she ran her fingers over his rock-hard biceps. "You're so strong," she whispered.

"You're so soft," he whispered back. His fingers slid down her waist to squeeze and stroke her bottom.

"I should be all muscular like you."

"You sound just like Z's sub. Listen, sweetling, and I'll tell you again. I know it's not politically correct, but I like my women soft." He pulled her closer. "And curvy." He skimmed a hand over her waist and then teased her breast until she sighed with pleasure. "And responsive. I love your body, little sub." He pressed a kiss to her fingers.

His women—and she was one of them? The thought made her warm inside.

And he liked her the way she was—God, how awesome was that—someone who looked like him lusted after her body. Tilting her head, she watched him fondle her breasts, his lips curved in a smile, his eyes half-lidded.

She really did have nice breasts, didn't she?

And if he kept up his attentions, she was going to get all turned on again. How did he *do* that? She ran her fingers down his neck, tracing along his jaw.

Cupping one breast, he rubbed his thumb over the nipple. "Now tell me"—his voice changed from lazy indulgence to a deeper, firmer timbre—"how did you feel when you were tied and opened for my pleasure?"

Her hand stopped midstroke. *Talk about it?* He wanted to talk about...that? Men weren't supposed to be so verbal, were they?

"Shy, little sub? After all that I've done to you? I've had my fingers buried in your pussy, my mouth on your clit, my cock rammed inside you. If you can let me do that, surely you can talk to me."

Heat seared her cheeks, and he chuckled. "Did being tied up scare you?"

She nodded, turned to hide her face in his shoulder.

He rose on one elbow. Grasping her shoulder, he pressed her flat, securing her even further with a leg across her hips. "You don't hide your feelings from yourself or from me. Tell me how you felt when you were tied up."

"Vulnerable," she whispered. "Like I couldn't help what you were going to do."

"And it aroused you even more." His hand played with her breasts, circling the tightening nipples. "Kari? Did being so securely restrained arouse you? Did you like it?" He pinched one nipple, a tiny flash of pain-pleasure.

"Yes." She looked away from him, her face hot. "Yes, darn it."

"Yes, what?"

"Yes, Sir. I liked it."

"Brave girl." He kissed her gently, nibbling on her lips. "It's not easy to admit enjoying something so different from what our mamas said we should enjoy. Why they think everyone should be alike in making love when no one can even agree on what ice cream they like, I'll never know."

He rose, disappearing into the tiny bathroom in the corner. When he returned, he brought back a warm washcloth. Standing beside the bed, he wiped the sweat from her face.

"Thank you. That feels good." It also felt strange to have this giant guy being so nurturing. Especially since his leathers were still open and displaying everything.

He put his knee on the bed and leaned forward. What was he...? He parted her thighs, stroking between them to clean her...there.

Blushing furiously, she tried to close her legs. "I can do that."

"I enjoy doing this sometimes." His knee settled on her ankle to keep her legs apart. He was very thorough. She was squirming and everything down there tingled before he was done.

As he walked into the bathroom, the leathers molded to him, showing every hard curve of his butt and thighs.

She pushed herself up and sat on the side of the bed, her head whirling. How very different this was from anything she'd done before. His control of her was what she'd wanted, and so far past what she'd expected that it scared her. Had she really begged? Screamed? Come over and over?

He returned with another warm washcloth and handed it to her. "Since you feel left out, you can join in. Wash me, Kari." He stood in front of her, totally unselfconscious, totally gorgeous, his sex framed in the V of the opened front.

Wash him. She could do that. Would even enjoy doing that. Kneeling on the bed, she started with his testicles, so soft, so heavy in her hands. When done, she moved forward. His penis, even nonerect and wrinkly, was still huge. Thick. And under her fingers and the washcloth, it started to grow.

"Your hands feel good on me, little sub," he said. He lifted her chin and gazed down into her eyes, and his voice changed, deepened and hardened, much like his penis was hardening in her hand. "Put your mouth on me now." *His master voice.* "What do you say to me?"

He wanted her to—well, okay—she'd done it before. In bed. In the dark. He'd be able to see her. Watch her. *Oh God.*

She licked her lips. "Yes, Sir."

She dropped the washcloth onto the floor and then took his penis into her hands. Even as she held it, it hardened, lengthened. *Wow.*

"See what just your hands can do to me?" he murmured. "My body wants yours. My cock wants those sweet lips around it, your mouth sucking on it."

The thought was empowering. Exciting. Hauling in a breath, she licked up his erection like an ice-cream cone, letting her tongue trace the big veins running along the outside. The skin was all softness wrapped over an iron bar. She slid her lips over the velvety-soft head. He growled in pleasure when her tongue swirled around its edge, so she concentrated there for a while. Then she moved on, trying stuff, seeing what reactions she could get.

When she sucked all of him into her mouth, his breath stopped.

Her tongue up the underside of his penis made his stomach muscles jerk.

He stroked her hair. "You are very good at this, sweetie.

Pride surged through her. *Sex*. She could do it.

He murmured, "Tighten your lips just a little—no teeth, please. Now, up and down, fast, and hard."

She did, and did it darned well, she knew, as his hand closed convulsively in her hair.

"Damn, but you have a wonderful mouth." A minute later, he said, "Stop now."

She looked up at him in surprise. He smiled down at her, traced her wet lips with his finger. "Don't worry, sweetheart, we'll finish later. For now, it's time to return downstairs. Master Z asked a few of the regulars in to demonstrate the equipment. Of course, compared to a normal bondage night, the scenes will be relatively mild."

She nodded.

"Go use the bathroom while I pick out your clothes."

Let him pick out her clothing? *No way*. She'd seen pictures of what people wore in fetish clubs. "No. I have clothes here, and I'll —" At the sight of his darkening eyes, she stopped, closed her mouth. *Too late*. She'd seen that look on his face with Sally, with herself.

"Little sub, you have exceeded my patience. Five swats." Gripping her wrists, he pulled her off the bed and took her place. He didn't release her. "Bend over my knees."

She tried to back away and got nowhere. "No." She shook her head frantically, her heart starting to hammer in her chest.

"No?" He lifted his brows in surprise. "Seven swats." His mouth set in a straight line, and the humor and gentleness disappeared from his face.

"Sir, please. No. You can't."

"I can. Ten."

No. She didn't resist—much—as he positioned her beside his knees. His grip unyielding, he laid her across his lap until her top half dangled on one side, her legs on the other. Her head spun, and she gasped. This wasn't happening, couldn't be—

"Farther, little sub," he said and shifted her until her bottom stuck up in the air. One of his legs pinned hers, and his left hand pressed her shoulders down. Trying to squirm, she realized she couldn't.

She felt his warm hand on her bare bottom, massaging, stroking. This wasn't a spanking, she thought, confusion running through her as her skin grew more sensitive to his touch. She felt the reawakening of desire.

And then he spanked her.

The first slap stung, and she jolted in disbelief. "No!" She wiggled, trying to escape.

He held her in place easily. "One."

Another slap. The sound echoed in the room as she jerked, the burning on her bottom intense and painful. "Two."

The third and fourth came almost together, hard and fast. Then slower, alternating cheeks. By eight, tears dripped from her eyes.

"Ten. There, little sub, all done." He didn't release her as he stroked her stinging cheeks. His hand was cool against the heat, bringing pain—and unexpected pleasure.

She lay limp, head hanging down, letting him pet her. Soothing her, she thought.

Slowly the strokes became longer. His hand cupped her cheeks, delving between her buttocks. One finger slid down into the crack, then farther, and animal hunger roused within her.

"Wa—" She clamped her mouth tight, her hands fisting in the carpet.

"You're learning, little sub, you're learning." He sounded infuriatingly amused.

Then he slid her legs apart, opening her to his touch, and his fingers moved through her tender, sensitive folds, swirling over her clitoris. His fingers slid easily—she was very wet—awakening every nerve ending to burning arousal.

She moaned. The stinging pain of her bottom somehow increased the need flaring in her.

As she squirmed under the onslaught, he chuckled and, pinning her hips with one hand, plunged two fingers inside her.

"Ahhh!" An unbearable storm of sensation exploded inside her, and she came hard, bucking uncontrollably against his thrusts.

Before she had recovered, he picked her up off his knees and turned her into his embrace, handling her as if she weighed nothing.

"Shhh," he murmured, his cheek pressed to her hair. He kissed her wet cheeks and took her mouth so gently and sweetly that she started crying again. Not speaking, he just held her, stroking her with the same hand that had spanked her and then given her an incredible orgasm.

Exhaustion claimed her. Her muscles went limp. He held her firmly against his chest, and there was a strange security in his powerful arms.

She finally pulled in a shuddering breath. "Sir?"

He kissed the top of her head. "Learn to think before you speak, little sub. Not every Dom is as easygoing as I am."

She stiffened. Easygoing?

He chuckled and stroked her hair. "Of course, some subs mouth off just to get punished. Amazing how much fun a good spanking can be, isn't it? I sure don't remember that being covered in my college classes."

A gulping laugh broke from her, and she took a breath as the world returned to normal. "Um, Sir? What do you do for a living? You never said."

"Neither did you."

Well, they were definitely better acquainted today. "I'm a biology teacher. High school."

"Lucky kids. I'm a cop. A detective, actually. Want to see my handcuffs?"

She shook her head no and then rubbed her cheek over the

springy hair on his chest. "No wonder you intimidated Buck so easily."

A growl rumbled through him. "He's lucky he got off so lightly."

"Sir?"

"Um-hmm?"

His arms never loosened, she was still snuggled up against him, held so firmly she couldn't move. The fact she found that reassuring was a little frightening. "When Buck grabbed me, you told him it was my choice whether to leave or not. But you didn't give me a choice now. You grabbed me...and spanked me."

"Ah." He rubbed his chin on the top of her head. "Your wannabe Dom lost his temper and tried to make you do something you didn't want. You didn't have a safe word arranged, did you?"

"Well, no. But—"

"Now I could be mistaken, but earlier, I told you what I planned to do. Did I mention spanking?"

"But I didn't say yes."

"Ah, sweetie, what I heard was that you didn't say *no*." His fingers cupped her cheek, raised her face to look at him. His brown eyes seemed to bore right into her. "I felt your body's response. First in the bar and again here. Was I mistaken?"

Heat flooded her cheeks. "No," she whispered. He'd barely touched her down below and she'd climaxed. Hard.

"Brave girl." His voice was warm, lazy, as comforting as his hands stroking her shoulders. "One other thing. Did I lose my temper?"

"Well." He'd been...displeased, definitely. But his voice and actions had been carefully controlled, she realized with surprise. Her lesson had been very deliberate. "No, Sir."

"Ah." He ran his fingers down her arm to her hand, massaged her palm. "Being under someone's control and punished... Some people find that very erotic, especially if you're already aroused."

He lifted her hand, sucked on a finger, and the feeling of his mouth anywhere on her body made her pussy clench. "You are one of those people who find it erotic, Kari. If you didn't, you'd have used your safe word."

She stayed silent. Nothing in her life was ever going to be quite the same again, was it? What she'd found out about herself these two evenings... She had some hard thinking to do. Soon.

When she didn't answer, he hugged her tightly, then set her on her feet. He steadied her as her knees wobbled. When his hands rubbed across her still-stinging bottom, she hissed.

He actually chuckled, the jerk. "You won't forget again, now will you? Because I could grow fond of seeing your pretty ass turn red under my hand."

"No, Sir, I won't forget."

"Very good." His eyes roamed over her body. From the heavy-lidded stare, the flush on his skin, and the thick wedge of flesh bulging under his leathers, she could tell he had enjoyed punishing her.

He moved a little closer. He was close, very close. His vest hung open, exposing a hard six-pack of abdominal muscles. "I could easily... No, I better not. Use the bathroom and take a quick shower." He grinned. "You need it now, I'm afraid. I'll pick out your clothes."

Her mouth opened, closed quickly, and she just nodded.

Pleased, he pressed a quick kiss to each breast, making her breath catch. "Go."

CHAPTER TEN

Dan listened to the shower as he opened the armoire door and surveyed his choices. Z kept a nice variety of fetish wear in each room. He eyed a French corset and then shook his head. She wasn't ready for that one—not yet—although those breasts would look sensational pushed up and overflowing. His cock twitched in agreement.

Maybe a maid's outfit? No. She was a modest woman, and he'd pushed her hard. He could relent with the clothing. *A bit.*

He pulled a dress out, soft and clinging, with a halter top that tied behind the neck. Anything that tied was fun. And the midthigh length was long enough to give her a sense of security. He grinned. That wouldn't last.

Perhaps he should keep her up here? But no. She'd come to the Shadowlands for an introduction to the lifestyle, so she really should see some of the regulars play. Considering how she'd reacted so far, it might be interesting.

She was so sweet.

He smiled, remembering her wide-eyed look when he told her to suck him, the tears on her cheeks after her spanking. *Sweet. Innocent.* Some men liked battling with sarcastic, angry subs. He wasn't one of them. Although he appreciated her courage and sparking temper, her modesty and nurturing nature drew him even more.

Her responses were so compelling, so honest, that he found himself wanting to wring more from her. But he needed to control himself to keep from pushing her too fast and far. She wouldn't stop with this visit. She might retreat after this, but her true nature was submissive. Now that she'd discovered the depth of passion inside her, vanilla sex would be even more tasteless to her.

She stepped out of the shower, rosy pink from the heat, her shoulders a confection above the blue towel. *Yum*. Crossing the room, he bent his head to nibble the curve where her neck met her shoulder. He tilted her head back and kissed the softness of her neck. "You taste wonderful and smell divine."

"Thank you," she said. She'd obviously recovered her composure in the shower, and her little shivers were gone completely.

Back in control, was she? Hmmm.

"I found something you'll like," he said, stripping the towel from her. "It slides right over your head."

Kari paused at the top of the stairs. The noise from the bar washed over her, bringing back a semblance of reality.

Why was she still here? She'd achieved her goal, to see what this BDSM stuff was all about. Now she really wanted to think about what had happened, what she'd done—what he'd done—for a while. A long while. She needed to be away from here to do that.

Time to go home. Her body was satisfied. Oh yes, more satisfied than ever in her life.

She turned to look at Master Dan and caught her breath when the soft material of the dress rubbed against her tender nipples.

No bra. No panties. She would have horrified the nuns. Then again, considering the other clothing in the armoire, she should be grateful this dress covered her fully. She'd seen a sheer lacy gown in there with the breasts and groin cut out. Good grief.

Yes, she appreciated this dress. This amount of indecency was enough for her. And Master Dan had refused to allow her underwear. She'd never gone—what did they call it?—*commando* before, and the cold air touching her nether regions made her feel very naked down there.

A little excited too, but she'd die before admitting that.

"I think I'll go home now," she said as he moved closer and tucked a firm arm around her waist.

He tilted his head and studied her silently. Unexpectedly, his fingers stroked across her breasts, and she sucked in a breath at the tingling, inside and out.

"No, little sub, your body isn't ready to leave yet." He held out his hand. "Take my hand."

It was an order, and her fingers were in his grip before she thought about saying no.

His eyes softened, and when he smiled approval, she had to smile back. He was right, darn him. The part of her that knew better, that followed the rules, wanted to leave. All the rest of her wanted to stay, to have his arm around her waist, to do what he ordered her to do.

He led her downstairs to the bar. Boy, things had livened up. Men and women nodded at him, greeted him by name. Not all of them, though. Where there were couples, only one would speak. The dominant one, whether man or woman. A few people were at the bar; others occupied the couches, occasionally with a man or woman at their feet. An older woman in an evening gown sat at a table with a male sub kneeling beside her.

She noticed the roped-off areas near the walls had been brightly lit, standing out in the shadowy room. She frowned and tugged him in the direction of one. "What—" At his narrowed gaze, she gulped. "Sir?"

"Good catch." And when he grinned, the flash of white in his tanned face was mesmerizing. "You have questions for me, Kari?"

"Yes, Sir."

"Ask."

But her questions disappeared right out of her mind when the roped-off area came into sight.

A naked woman squirmed on the St. Andrew's cross.

Kari's mouth dropped open. Good God. In the class, Master Raoul had put a clothed man up there; this was so very different. She took a step back, came up against Master Dan's hard frame.

His arm came around her, his hand just under her breast. He whispered in her ear, "Imagine yourself up there, unable to cover yourself, open to every man's gaze, available to every man's touch."

She could...she could see herself, and the thought was terrifying. *Erotic*. Her pussy dampened, and he rumbled a laugh in her ear. "Yes, the thought excites you, doesn't it?"

No way, no way would she let herself be put in that position. She shivered as he set his hand almost on her pubis, pressing her back against his erection.

"I would like to see you there too. But not yet, my sweet."

Hand against her back, he moved through the room. They passed a naked woman on the spiderweb, and then a man on the bondage table. A hooded Domme in a red latex corset stood beside him, wielding a switch.

When they reached the back wall, Kari stopped again. Her hands closed convulsively on Sir's hard biceps.

"What are they...she...?" But she could see. A woman lay on her stomach across the sawhorse, her wrists cuffed to the front legs. Her bent knees were strapped to the short cushions on each side, and she showed...everything, even more than the woman on the wall frame.

A man stood behind her, his jeans open, fully erect. He thrust into the woman with one stroke, and she screamed in pleasure.

Master Dan had to pull Kari away, she was so outraged. "Sir, he just took her right there. In front of everyone."

He stopped, lifted her chin, and looked her right in the eyes. "Call me Master Dan or Master. I tire of being nameless. I want to hear my name and my title from your soft lips, little sub."

"Bu—"

His eyes darkened, his mouth tight. He was really, really serious. *Call him Master*. To actually say that *aloud* felt like she'd be giving him too much power over her.

He waited, fingers unyielding, his other hand clamped on her shoulder. People swirled past around them. A woman somewhere broke into a cry of rapture, a man shouted in pain.

She had let him tie her and take her, punish her. Her body recognized his title, even if she didn't want to admit it. "Master."

"Again."

"Master Dan." As she feared, saying the words relinquished something inside her, some control she'd still been holding on to.

"Sweetly done, little Kari." He took her lips gently, lovingly even, his tongue rubbing against hers, slow and sensuous, until she was pressing up against him for more. His arms tightened around her. He was hard and ready, and she wanted him again. When she rubbed her breasts against his chest in invitation, he growled a laugh, and his hands reached under her skirt to massage her bottom.

The air on her butt hit her like a cold shower; she pushed away and opened her mouth to scold him. Shut her mouth.

"Nice save." He held her against his chest, stroking her hair. "What should you see next?" He glanced over at the other side of the room and shook his head. "Mmmph, not that."

She stood on tiptoe and still couldn't see.

"Perhaps next time." He stroked her cheek and smiled down into her eyes. "There will be a next time, will there not?"

Oh my God. Come back? This was so much more intense than just that first lesson. And seeing the equipment in use... Just look at what might be done to her. "Uh—"

His eyebrows drew together. “The answer is, ‘yes, Sir.’”

“Yes, Sir.” He wanted her to come back. More. Oh God.

“I think we both deserve a drink, don’t you?” he murmured and pulled her to the bar.

“Daniel, how’re things at the station?” A white-haired man, his hands knotty with arthritis, nodded at Sir. “Did I hear Bonner is retiring?”

“End of next year, he says.” Sir shook the old man’s hand with obvious care. “Master Gerald, this is Kari, here for the newbie classes.”

“Pleased to meet you, Kari.” Gerald wrapped an arm around the tiny woman standing next to him. “This is my wife, Martha.”

Probably in her seventies, Martha wore a collar and cuffs that matched her bright pink bustier. Her long black skirt had pink studs along the waist and hem. She nodded at Kari, her aged eyes dancing with humor. “Master?”

“Go ahead,” the old man said.

“Welcome to the club, Kari. We enjoy seeing young faces.”

Was she allowed to talk? Kari glanced up at Sir, received a nod. “Thank you. I’m pleased to meet you.”

“Kari, you’re still here!”

Kari turned to see Jessica break away from a group of people. “May I borrow your sub for a moment, Master Dan?” she asked, taking Kari’s hand.

Sir frowned, pointed to a spot about ten feet away. “Go no farther than that.”

Jessica dragged her over to the spot. “How on earth did you end up with Master Dan again? I heard what happened Monday when you left.”

Gossip. Like cockroaches, it survived in any climate and apparently any kink. Kari grinned. “He decided he wanted another night. Go figure.”

Jessica pulled at her lip and watched Sir talk to the old man for a moment before turning her gaze back to Kari. "Well, that's interesting. Are you doing all right?"

Kari sucked in a breath. "It's so different. I like it and I don't want to like it, and I feel like I'm going straight to hell, you know?"

Jessica laughed. "I doubt we'll get a chance to chat tonight. Your last class is Saturday, right? Why don't you come early, and we'll have time to talk."

"I'd like that very much."

"See you then." Jessica grinned and darted away, heading for the front of the room.

As Kari rejoined Sir, Cullen walked over, his grin breaking the hardness of his face. "How's your sub, Dan?"

Master Dan stroked his hand down her cheek, his approval of her so obvious that she unconsciously leaned into his hand. Both men smiled. "How do you think?"

Master Cullen studied her, his eyes lingering on her mouth, and she realized her lips were swollen from Master Dan's kisses, from sucking on his... She flushed hotly.

"She looks nicely used." He set two drinks on the bar top, and Master Dan handed her one.

She sipped. Rum and Diet Coke.

"Master Cullen never forgets a drink." Sir's finger traced over her wet lips. When she closed her lips around his finger and sucked, he chuckled, though his eyes heated. "He rarely forgets a sub's reaction or needs; he's very popular." He tapped her drink. "Enjoy it while you can."

That sounded ominous, and she edged away from him as she sipped. The strong drink gave her a slight buzz. No supper. Oops.

When she'd finished about half, Master Dan smiled at her and pulled her a little closer. She realized his eyes weren't smiling... No, he had that look in his eyes, the one that made her quiver inside. "I have decided your lessons are not over for the night."

She froze, then remembered to swallow.

"Your body is mine for tonight. Is that what we agreed, little sub?" He waited. "Kari?"

"Yes, M-Master."

"I use your body as I please." He waited for her nod, then leaned forward and whispered, "And give it where I please."

Her eyes widened, but he already had her hands in his. "One of the reasons that subs wear cuffs in here is this—" He hooked the cuffs together, then pulled a chain down from the low rafter over the bar area. Lifting her arms up, he hooked the cuffs to the chain. And stepped back.

Her arms were fastened straight over her head. She yanked, couldn't move. Her breath came fast, and her heart pounded. "Master?"

"Oh, very good." He smiled, nuzzled her face, his jaw abrasive with a day's whiskers.

"I don't—"

"Kari, a few minutes ago, you showed me that being looked at by strangers is arousing to you. Even being touched..." He tugged on the strings holding her halter top up.

The top dropped, leaving her naked above the waist. In a roomful of people. Many—heck, most—of whom were men. Cool air wafted across her breasts, and she shivered.

She shook her head. "Master Dan. No. Please, no," she whispered frantically. She pulled again at the chain.

"You'll only hurt your wrists," Master Dan murmured and bit her chin, the little nip almost painful. "If you damage those pretty wrists, I'll punish you." His hand reached under her skirt, right in front of everyone, and rubbed her naked bottom as a reminder. "Use your safe word—or stop pulling."

She stopped, hoping he'd take his hand away, but he continued to play with her butt, sliding his finger into the crack, squeezing her sore cheeks. At his teasing touches, pain, then pleasure surged through her.

Her nipples tightened, attracting his attention. He moved his hands up to fondle them, pulling gently, pinching until the nipples stood erect. Embarrassment vied with growing arousal within her.

"There. I think you're ready for visitors, don't you?" He turned her so she faced the room rather than the bar. Her legs shook, and the chains chimed softly over her head. He exchanged a look with the bartender.

"I do enjoy that sound," the bartender commented. "She has gorgeous breasts; you must be pleased."

Master Dan nodded. "I am. She's incredibly responsive." He rubbed his knuckles over one breast, and it tightened again to a hard, almost painful nub.

As Kari felt heat rush into her face, Master Cullen laughed. "A beautiful reaction. Love the way she turns red."

After kissing the top of her head, Master Dan moved a couple of feet away to sit on a bar stool, leaving her standing by herself. When he turned his head to talk with a friend, she tried to shift around to face the bar.

"Stay where I put you, little sub."

She did. Even when a man walked right up to her. He wore black leathers with gold trim like Sir's—another dungeon monitor. He glanced at Master Dan.

"Good to see you, Sam." Sir nodded at him. "She's one of the beginners."

Despite his silvery gray hair, the man had muscles like a young man. He looked at her and his eyes were pale blue in a stern, leathery face. "I couldn't help but admire your tits. What's your name, girl?"

If she didn't look at him, didn't answer, maybe he'd go away. Instead, he caught her chin just like Master Dan and leaned down. His eyes were piercing. Unforgiving. "Subs answer questions put to them. What is your name?"

"Kari. Sir," she whispered.

Without releasing her chin, he stroked one hand over a breast, squeezing it, pulling on the nipple hard enough that she had to catch her breath. She didn't know him at all, and he was playing with her. He could do anything to her right now, and he knew it. The thought was horrifying. *Exciting.* She felt herself moisten down below and pressed her thighs together. *Oh God.*

He'd watched her face as he touched her, and now he smiled. "There's a good girl." Running a finger down her cheek, he walked away, leaving her confused. *Needy.*

Master Dan studied her, and his hard lips curved in a faint smile. His gaze softened, but when she looked at him in appeal, he shook his head. "Not yet, Kari."

He turned back to his conversation. She closed her eyes, felt the trickle of her own arousal down her leg. This was so... She couldn't...

A hand grabbed her breast, and she gasped and opened her eyes. A man her age dressed in a black suit, the cruel-eyed beginner. His fingers twisted her breast.

Biting back a cry, Kari tried to pull back.

She heard a low growl, and Sir ripped the man away from her.

Hands fisted in the man's suit, Master Dan held him up in the air as if he were a child. Sir's face was furious. Terrifying. "Did you ask permission to touch my sub?"

Not waiting for an answer, he shook the man. Hard. The man's head bobbled as he gasped, "Sorry, sorry. I—"

With a snarl of disgust, Master Dan dropped him onto the floor. A DM ran up, and Sir scowled at him.

"Sorry, Dan. He got away from me while I dealt with another newbie." Grabbing the suited man by the scruff of his neck, the DM pulled him away. Quickly.

Kari didn't blame him. When Master Dan turned to her, she cringed at the look in his eyes, the threat in his pose.

He stopped. Taking a deep breath, he visibly relaxed his muscles. She could see the violence flow out of him. Suddenly he was back to the Master Dan she knew—well, didn't know—but at least he didn't look like he'd tear people apart anymore.

Very gently, he unhooked her from the chain and wrapped his arms around her. She nestled there, feeling small, scared. *Comforted.* He simply held her, not moving, just letting her quiver in his arms.

When she stopped shaking, he ran his hands up and down her back. “I’m sorry, sweetie. Some beginners don’t remember the rule that no one touches a sub without their Dom’s permission.”

He cupped her face, his gaze intent. “I should have been more careful with you. Can you forgive me?”

The man took her breath away. Did he know how rare it was to hear an honest admission of fault and apology? “I forgive you, Master.”

He gave her a warm smile, but his eyes still held remorse. He felt horrible about what had happened, and that just seemed wrong. He’d grabbed the man within a second. He shouldn’t feel so bad.

She put her hand on his and wrinkled her nose at him. “But I forgive only if I get a kiss to make it all better, Sir.”

The remorse lifted from his eyes like fog from a mountain. Mischief took its place, and he grinned.

She gave him a wary glance. He had an appalling habit of ignoring respectable behavior.

His hand traced across her breast. “He touched you here, I think.” He bent to kiss the spot. His lips feathered against her skin. “And here.” He lifted the other breast for his lips to nuzzle.

Her nipples tightened into hard points as she started the slow glide back into need.

He touched her lower, cupping her mound. “I’m beginning to regret he didn’t lay a hand elsewhere.”

Right there in front of everyone, he had his hands on her...her private parts. But even as she flushed and scowled at him, her pelvis tilted into his hand.

His brows lowered, his mouth flattened. “Did you just frown at me?”

CHAPTER ELEVEN

She froze. Oh no no no.

He waited, tilted his head.

"Yes, Master. I'm sorry, Master. Very sorry, Master."

Amusement glittered in his eyes, even though his face remained stern. "Well, now, I can't have a sub giving me frowns. My reputation will be ruined." His hands closed around her wrists, and a second later, he'd hooked her cuffs to the overhead chains. Again.

She barely kept the scowl from reappearing on her face, and he could tell. The jerk.

He chuckled, then hauled her into his arms long enough to take her lips so thoroughly she sagged from the chains when he released her. "Ah, now that's better."

He resumed his seat, but he didn't take his eyes off her this time. No one was going to sneak up again without him noticing. And somehow, that just wasn't helping her feel much better. People stared at her, much like she'd looked at the woman on the cross. The men's eyes ranged down her body, lingering on her breasts.

She tried to keep her attention on Sir, watching as he talked quietly with the club members and other DMs. He discussed sports with one, advised another on disciplining a sub, argued politics. Everyone liked him, obviously, although he certainly wasn't as gregarious as Cullen or Raoul.

No one came over until... Her eyes widened.

The owner of the Shadowlands, Master Z, approached, strolling through the crowd like a lion walking through a forest of prey. Shoot, *all* the dungeon monitors moved like that, had that aura of power and self-confidence. And Master Z was coming here.

Her breath hitched. She was all but naked.

He stopped beside Master Dan. "You didn't break him into pieces, Daniel. I appreciate your restraint."

"Came close." Master Dan's frown was intense. "My fault. I should have been more aware."

"Indeed. A lesson for all concerned." Master Z's gaze turned to Kari, and she felt a flush sweep all the way from her breasts to her face. He glanced at Master Dan.

Sir not only nodded, he actually grinned.

Master Z moved close enough she could feel his warmth, see the pleasure in his silvery eyes when he looked at her. "You are as lovely as I had thought, Kari." His smile made her feel warm, welcome. *Beautiful.*

"And I see you have found favor with our Master Dan." He stroked a hand down her cheek. "He didn't know it, but he has been looking for a gentle heart, a caring spirit, one who needed his control to discover the full depth of her passion. You are well suited."

Her head spun as she tried to comprehend his words, but when he rubbed his knuckles over each breast in turn, studied the way they hardened, he derailed her thoughts completely. "You'll be the envy of the Doms, Dan," he said. With another smile for her, he strolled back into the crowd.

"Bloody matchmaker," the bartender said with a grin, refilling Master Dan's glass from a bottle of spring water.

Two lines appeared between Master Dan's brows, and his mouth tightened. "He's full of it and wasting his time to boot. I'm not looking for any matches." His mouth thinned when he looked at Kari.

Kari felt cold creeping into her. Even though he was still right there, the man she'd been with earlier had disappeared. She felt abandoned and very vulnerable with her hands chained over her head. She bit her lip and looked down, away, anywhere but at his cold eyes.

"Hell." Something thumped on the bar, and then boots appeared in her line of sight. A hand lifted her chin, warm against her skin. "I'm sorry, sweetie. I might be annoyed with Z, but that has nothing to do with you." He kissed her gently, and tears burned her eyes. "You've brought me only pleasure tonight."

"Are you sure?" she whispered. He hadn't frowned at Master Z, only at her.

"I'm a cold bastard inside." He ran a finger down her cheek, his eyes crinkling at the corners when he smiled. "And you're very warm. Yes, I'm sure." His hand stroked down her body to circle her breast, lower still to cup her mound. With his other hand, he raised her skirt and touched her intimately, sliding his fingers through her wet folds. She gasped as pleasure surged through her. He kissed her neck, then bit her sharply. His finger pressed against her pussy, undoubtedly feeling it clench in reaction to the erotic thrill. "Definitely warm," he murmured, licking the bite. "Hot might be a better word."

She flushed. Although it was a heady feeling being called hot, she knew everyone could see where his hand lingered. To her relief and disappointment, he kissed her nose and settled himself back on the bar stool. "I'll finish my drink and then let you down." He took a small sip—way too small; they'd be here all night—and smiled at her.

She managed, barely, not to glare at him.

He lifted his eyebrows, lips quirking in amusement, then turned as another man in gold-trimmed leathers walked up. The mean-looking one she'd seen with Raoul earlier. "Dan."

"Nolan, I heard you were back. Welcome home," Master Dan said, shaking the man's hand. "The place wasn't the same without you."

"It's good to be back in the States." The stranger tilted his head at Kari, and Sir nodded permission.

Nolan approached and looked down at her. Did all these dungeon monitor guys have to be so big? Black hair and black eyes as if he had Hispanic or Native American ancestry. His cold, hard gaze and the threatening set of his mouth made her want to flee. Involuntarily, she yanked on her restraints, tried to back up.

He didn't move, just watched her futile struggles. Her breath kept getting faster.

"Do you like being touched?" His voice was low and harsh with a hint of a Texan accent.

Her hands clenched on the chains. She couldn't answer that, not out loud. She licked her lips, glanced sideways at Sir.

Master Dan's eyes narrowed. "Answer the question, Kari. Honestly."

The man's eyes were so scary that she dropped her gaze to the floor. "Yes, Sir, I do," she whispered miserably. How could she want Master Dan's hands on her so badly and still be turned on by someone else's touch?

"Well, I'd hate to disappoint such an honest sub," the man drawled. She looked up. His mouth curved slightly, amusement in his eyes. Maybe, maybe he wouldn't hurt her—

He did worse. He tormented her, fondling her breasts with callused hands, circling around the edges of her nipples until the nubs burned with need. He finally relented and expertly squeezed each nipple to just the edge of pain and pleasure.

Her back arched, and she couldn't muffle a moan.

At that, the man actually smiled. He tapped her on the cheek with a scarred finger, slapped Master Dan on the shoulder, and walked away.

To her horror, Kari felt wetness running down her inner thighs, and she pressed her legs together.

Master Dan studied her. Nodded. "Looks like we need to go upstairs again."

He released her hands with a quick twist, and she staggered against him. Her lower half actually ached with need.

But rather than walking toward the steps they'd used before, he headed toward the back. Past the sawhorses.

A new woman was on one, her bottom poking up and out. Kari slowed, inhaled sharply. The woman's crotch had been completely shaved. *Oh my*.

Master Dan wrapped his arms around Kari from behind, held her in place when she would have hurried to get past. He set his chin on her shoulder, seeing everything she was seeing. "Shaving your pussy makes it more sensitive. To everything," he whispered in her ear. "And the spanking bench puts that little pussy where all of it can be reached. Touched. Played with."

His hand dipped down, stroked her folds right through her dress, his fingers knowledgeable. Between his seductive words and his penetrating fingers, she couldn't control the tremor of arousal that ran through her.

"Yes, I think you would like that position, little sub."

Her breath stopped entirely. *No—not in front of people*.

Just then, a man walked up to the woman on the sawhorse. He pulled her cheeks apart farther, slid two well-lubricated fingers into her anus, in and out, and everyone in the area heard the woman's moan.

Kari's knees gave out, and Master Dan swooped her up with a laugh. "Upstairs for you."

And without even breathing hard, he carried her upstairs and into a different room. Candlelight flickered over dark gray walls and black carpeting. No bed, only an armoire in the corner and a big easy chair in the other corner.

Still carrying her, Master Dan turned a little farther.

Kari stiffened in his arms. *A sawhorse*. Straps everywhere.

"You enjoyed looking; let's see if you enjoy riding." He put her on her feet and wrapped an arm around her, setting his big hand on her stomach to steady her. Grabbing her dress with one hand, he yanked it over her head, leaving her naked.

Her anxiety increased as his hot gaze slid down her body. "Spread your legs, Kari."

Staring into his eyes, she eased her legs apart.

"More." When she complied, he anchored her in place with a firm hand on her bottom, then touched her intimately, sliding his fingers through her wetness, caressing her clitoris with long, slow strokes. She grabbed his arms, her fingers digging into his skin as he drove her higher and higher until her anxiety disappeared under the surging need.

"There we go," he murmured. He turned her to face the sawhorse. Pressing her hips into the edge, he ordered in her ear, "Bend over." His erection pressed into her buttocks as she bent, and she shivered, wanting him inside, thrusting...

His chest hard against her back, he flattened her onto the bench. The cold leather chilled her bare stomach, shocking her back to reality. When he clipped her wrist cuffs to the rings on the front legs, she felt like a trapped animal. Panicking, she jerked at the restraints.

He closed his hands on her arms, holding her firmly. "Stop now, sweetie. Are you in pain? Use the safe word if you need to."

She panted, pulled at her wrists.

"Kari, answer me."

His words finally registered. *Safe word*. She could make him stop anytime. The reminder helped, and she hauled in a slower breath. "I-I'm okay."

"Of course you are." Releasing her arms, he eased back. His

hands settled on her back, warm against her cold skin. Gently, he massaged her shoulders until she sighed and relaxed.

"That's better, little sub," he murmured and kissed her cheek. "I like you a little anxious, but not scared."

She'd barely decided she wasn't too anxious. Then he set her knee on the attached padded bench and strapped it down. Then the other leg, securing her in an almost doggy position. With her knees set more forward, more of her showed.

When air slid like chilled fingers against her moist private places, she tried to move her legs. Nothing happened. *Everything* was on display, and she couldn't move.

As if he could read her mind, he said in a low, husky voice, "Now you're open to me. Fully. To my eyes, my fingers, my lips."

She shivered, and yet the burn of arousal inside her heightened.

He was behind her, and she couldn't see what he was doing, no matter how she twisted. A door creaked open.

"Master?" Her voice shook. "Are you there?"

"I'm here, Kari. I'll never leave you alone if you're restrained." Something rustled, and she realized the creaking sound had been the armoire door.

"Let's see if I can't get your mind off all these worries." He knelt behind her, his hands rough on her bottom, spreading her as his thumbs roamed up and down her labia. She squirmed, made a noise, and he laughed.

And set his mouth on her.

"Ahhh!" She jumped, her legs wrenching against the straps.

Rubbing her folds gently between his fingers, he exposed her clitoris completely. He swirled his tongue around it so hard and quickly, she cried out again.

"You feeling a little warmer?" He inserted a finger, and her tissues were so swollen from his previous use, she could feel every inch going in. She clenched around him.

"I like how my finger feels inside you," he murmured, "but I know you'll enjoy something longer. This should fit about right."

She felt so vulnerable, unable to see or move, as he pushed something into her. Not his cock; this thing was cold. Her vagina spasmed around it, tried to push it out. He held it in place and then moved it slowly in and out. She was so wet, it glided easily.

All the way out, then back in, filling her fully until she moaned. But it wasn't enough, not quite. When he took it out, her legs quivered uncontrollably.

He chuckled, and then she felt his tongue lick up and over her clitoris, over and over. He lapped at her like a dog, his tongue flat. Her insides tightened; her clit hardened. Every little cell in her waited, waited for each excruciatingly arousing slide of his tongue.

"More," she moaned. "Please, Master."

As if in response, she heard a *click* and a buzzing sound. When he touched the vibrator to her swollen labia, she gasped.

With a firm stroke, he slid it all the way into her vagina, and everything inside her burst into fiery pleasure. And then he pulled her clitoris into his mouth, rubbing it firmly with his tongue. With her legs strapped down, she couldn't move her hips, and the exquisite sensations grew even stronger, building into a fireball of ecstasy exploding out from her center. She screamed as the convulsions engulfed her.

When he wiggled the vibrator inside her, another climax rolled over her before the first was even done.

With a sensual hum of satisfaction, he removed the vibrator, making her vagina spasm again and her legs jerk.

He stepped away, and she heard the crinkle of foil as he sheathed himself. She tried to tip her head to see but couldn't. Her wrists and legs were still shackled. His hands on her bottom made her jump. Rubbing her buttocks, he murmured, "Still a little pink from your punishment. Such a pretty ass. And your pussy is wet and pink and ready for me."

Before she realized what he intended, he thrust into her, thick and hard. She felt herself stretching inside as he speared all the way to her cervix.

She yelped, pulling against the straps, the cuffs. "Too big, Master. Please..."

He chuckled. "Compliments from my sub?" His shaft moved inside her. Painfully. He pressed one hard hand down on her bottom, holding her in place. "Don't move, sweetling; your body will adjust."

Her whole lower half throbbed as if he'd shoved all her insides over for his possession, filled her to bursting.

Ignoring her little whimpers, he leaned over, his chest hard and hot against her back as his hands cupped her dangling breasts. "They just fall into my hands like ripe fruit," he murmured, squeezing gently, and she shivered.

Strapped, impaled, flattened from his weight, and now her breasts pressed upward from his hard hands. Surrounded entirely. Something opened in her mind. As she surrendered completely to his will, brutal arousal shocked through her and every nerve in her body violently awakened. "Master." She panted. "Master, I need—"

"Shhh. Soon, little sub." His breath seared her shoulder as his rough fingers abraded her sensitive nipples. When he pinched the points between his fingers, jolts seared through her until she squirmed uncontrollably, trying to rub her clit against the table. *More, please, more*. She rolled her forehead on the leather.

Murmuring something against her back, he bit the nape of her neck, holding it between his teeth, sending chills down her arms.

And then he finally, finally started to move, sliding his cock out of her so gradually, it seemed to take forever, then back in, an excruciatingly slow, circular motion. Her hands fisted on the straps as her body shook with unfulfilled need. Moaning, wanting more, faster, harder. She wiggled uncontrollably.

He pressed an unyielding hand against her butt, holding her in place and eliminating even the tiny movements she could make.

"Little sub, you're so tight and slick, you're threatening my control."

His speed increased slowly, too slowly, and she tried to raise her butt, but she couldn't do anything. Whatever he wanted to do to her, she had to take it.

The thought sent her over, and she came with a fast rush, writhing against the leather of the sawhorse.

His hand stroked down her back as he straightened a little. "No, that was an inadequate climax, sweetie," he said, massaging her buttocks.

He wanted more from her. She wasn't sure whether to cheer or cry.

"You'll give me a better one," he said with certainty. Then he pressed his hips against her, thrusting deeply, and she moaned, his size no longer painful, just incredibly pleasurable.

With a low laugh, he pulled out, then rammed into her and continued, withdrawing, then burying himself. Hard, fast. His balls slapped against her swollen labia. His thickness inside her was thrilling. Sensation built on sensation until her vagina tightened around him.

He shifted slightly, and suddenly his fingers were on her, sliding in her wetness all over her oversensitized clitoris. The overload was too much and everything contracted and convulsed inside her, and she was coming so violently that she screamed over and over.

With a final thrust so hard that he actually moved the sawhorse, he came too, and the hot jerks of his penis spasmed against her insides again and again until only twitches remained.

He rested against her, his breathing controlled and hard. She could feel his heart pounding against her back.

"Now *that* was a worthy climax," he said, his voice even deeper than normal. He kissed her shoulders, her neck, before pulling back.

As he withdrew, sliding out of her acutely sensitive tissues, she shuddered. After disappearing into the bathroom briefly, he undid her restraints, then removed her wrist cuffs. With careful hands, he helped her dismount and held her up when her legs wouldn't work.

"There now," he murmured in his rough voice. A soothing voice. Why did she feel so...so vulnerable now, like she'd break into tears any minute?

Cupping her chin with his hand, he tilted her face up. She blinked frantically against the burning in her eyes.

"Ah, baby." He picked her up, cradling her like a child, and oh, she needed that so badly. Cuddling her close, he sat down in the chair with her pressed against his chest.

She let her head drop onto his shoulder. Heard her breath hitch as she tried not to cry.

Holding her firmly, he rocked the chair and talked to her, his voice a low, soothing murmur, filling the empty spaces that had opened inside her. "You are a beautiful woman, Kari... I love that soft, rosy body of yours... You have such a gentle spirit... I am grateful that you trusted me enough to give in to what was inside you. All that passion, sweetheart, you shared with me... Do you know how beautiful you are when you show me your need and when you come without hiding anything?"

Not asking her for any response, he just continued talking, telling her of his pleasure, his pride in her, until the horrible feeling of vulnerability dissipated and she felt like she was herself again.

When she sighed, his arms tightened around her, and he kissed the top of her head. They rocked quietly for a few minutes, the silence warm. She'd never felt so close to anyone in her life.

Eventually, her brain turned back on with an almost audible click.

Her brain wasn't happy.

She felt...funny. Like too much had happened, like the world wasn't what she'd thought. *She* wasn't who she thought.

"Tell me," he said quietly, cupping her face. He kissed her temple, ruffling the tiny hairs with his breath. He snuggled her closer, his body warm where she was starting to feel cold. "Kari?"

"This isn't me," she whispered. "I'm not like this."

"Like what, sweetie?"

"I'm a teacher. I'm educated and smart. People don't boss me around."

"Ah, that. Being smart, educated, even having authority at work has nothing to do with what you like to do in private or in bed, sweetheart." He stroked her cheek, tucked her hair out of her sweat-streaked face. Wiped the tears running down her cheeks. She was crying?

"In your case, I figure you have three reasons that vanilla sex doesn't work for you. First, you really are submissive, for whatever reason. Some think it's just part of a person's personality, like being an introvert or extrovert. Others say it's upbringing. Doesn't really matter. You are what you are; you need what you need."

His words hit her almost like a sentence of doom: *You're submissive. There's no escape. Live with it.*

"Second, you, little nun, have guilt added into the mix. Your father's lectures, your religion disapproving of anything carnal—all inside you." He put his big hand between her breasts. "Right there."

She put her hand on top of his, could almost feel the big lump of judgments, criticism, scorn right under her ribs.

"And third, since you're an intelligent woman, your body wants to enjoy sex, but your brain never stops working and worrying." He rubbed her shoulder, stroked down her arm to take her hand. His fingers rubbed her knuckles. "Is that true, Kari?"

So true it was frightening. She could never stop thinking about what she should do, what he could do better, how hot the room was, what music was playing...

His dark brown eyes studied her face. When she sighed, he

nodded. "It's hard for an educated woman to turn her head off. That's part of the joy of being a submissive. None of the decisions are yours. When you can't refuse anything and can't even move, those voices in your head go silent. All you can do, and all you are permitted to do, is feel. And you felt everything, didn't you?"

She nodded, but he didn't need her answer. He'd known every little twitch she gave. She rubbed her cheek on his chest gratefully. Understanding why she'd reacted so strongly helped a little. A little.

She listened to the slow beat of his heart. Surrounded by his arms, his scent, her body relaxed into him. Something about his strength, his understanding, his concentrated focus on her and her needs, was almost too overwhelming. Refusing to think further, she burrowed closer and let herself float away.

Sometime later, a chime sounded. Master Dan shook her gently. "It's midnight, Cinderella, and the dance is over."

"What?" She blinked at him.

He helped her to her feet. Her legs shook. She looked up at him, feeling lost. His eyes softened, and he hugged her, kissing her deeply. Gently.

"I wish we had more time," he murmured. "But the DMs will be around soon to drag slowpokes out." He kissed her again, this time with his hand curled around the nape of her neck, holding her in place. "I'm going to go find your clothes. I'll be right back."

By the time she'd used the bathroom to freshen up, he had returned. After she dressed, he escorted her down the stairs.

"Hey, Dan!" Standing by the front door, a familiar-looking woman in a black bustier and leggings waved them over. Kari recognized the DM from Monday.

"Olivia," Master Dan said.

"Nice to see you using the private rooms again." Olivia gave Kari a disconcertingly slow and appreciative look before she turned back to Dan. "If you're interested, I'm throwing a dungeon party Sunday afternoon. Bring your pretty sub and come play."

"Ah—" Sir started.

"Don't say no. It's been far too long since you partied with us," the DM said. "We miss you."

Kari looked up. Surprise and what looked like guilt flickered in Master Dan's eyes. His muscular arm went rigid, then dropped away from her waist.

"I can't make it. Sorry." His voice sounded as if the life had drained out of it.

"Oh, honey, I'm sorry too." Olivia patted Sir's arm gently and moved away.

"Let's go," Master Dan said to Kari.

As she stepped out into the night, the humid air blanketed her, the scent of tropical flowers and swamp almost overpowering. The loss of Sir's touch created an ache inside her as he silently walked beside her to the tree-lined parking lot. Others were leaving also, faceless figures in the shadows and moonlight. Cars moved down the drive in a slow string of lights.

Taking her keys, he unlocked her car and opened the door. She looked up, hoping for a kiss, a hug...something...but his gaze was as remote as the distant moon.

"Thank you for the evening, Kari." His fingertips brushed her cheek, featherlight.

Her lips tightened. No more *sweetheart* from him. The ache increased, and she tightened her lips against a betraying quiver. He had only promised an evening. The evening was over, and she never caused scenes. All those etiquette lessons from the nuns hadn't gone to waste. She slid into the car, then forced a smile and a cool tone, "Thank you for the lesson, Master Dan. I do appreciate the time you've spent with me."

His eyes were distant, but sadness lingered in the lines of his face. "Drive carefully." He put her keys into her hand and closed the door softly.

CHAPTER TWELVE

Dan's chest ached like he'd cracked all his ribs. He rubbed his sternum as he walked back to the Shadowlands. Why Olivia's invitation had hit him so hard, he didn't know; after all, he'd been fending off well-meaning friends for three years now.

Fending off subs too. He remembered Kari's expression a minute ago, how her big eyes had filled with confusion, then hurt. His mouth tightened, and the frozen feeling inside him increased. Being with her a second time had been a mistake. For both of them. It wouldn't happen again.

Not bothering to knock, Dan walked into Z's office. "Got a minute?"

Z set down the paper he'd been reading. "Daniel. Did you have a good evening?"

"Fine." Dan raised his hand to run it through his hair, stopped halfway, and lowered his arm. Subs weren't the only people whom Z could read like a grade-school primer. "Just wanted to give you a heads-up. I won't be able to make the dinner on Friday or be here on Saturday."

"Is there a problem?"

"No." The terse answer with no explanation was rude, but he

had no damned explanation. Just that he needed to not be here for a while.

Z studied him for a minute before asking, "Was little Kari a disappointment to you?"

The damned mind-reading psychologist could be like a cat with a cornered mouse. "She'll make someone a wonderful sub, I'm sure. I'm not in the market for one, though, and you fucking well know it." He winced at the raw sound of his own voice.

"I hear you," Z said mildly. "Well, then. I'll tell Jessica about Friday. We'll miss you on Saturday, Daniel."

"Right." Mouth set tight, Daniel headed out, resisting the urge to slam the door behind him.

Outside, he scowled up at the moon, remembering how Kari's pale skin had glowed in its light. He shook his head. Real fucking romantic. He pulled his keys out, headed for his truck. No traffic, he'd be home soon enough.

Home. He sighed, rubbed his face. The thought of his cold, empty apartment made his guts twist. *Fine then.* He'd hit the station instead, put in some time on his unsolved cases stack.

Early Thursday morning, Kari wandered through her quiet neighborhood, a basket of warm muffins over her arm. Around five in the morning, she'd finally given up on any sleep and put the time to good use.

Tail waving in the air, her German shepherd, Prince, trotted in front of her, guarding her from evil field mice, stray cats, and other dogs. Especially the aggressive poodle that lived three houses down. A cool breeze brushed against her skin and sent droplets from last night's rain pattering off the leaves onto the pavement.

After getting home last night, she'd sat out on the patio, trying to come to terms with Master Dan's behavior. She'd felt so close to him, and he'd acted like he'd felt the same, and then he'd just shut down. But he'd warned her, after all, said he didn't have anything to give. She shook her head. He'd given her more than any man before, but apparently, she wasn't enough for him, not compared to his dead wife.

Kari stopped, closed her eyes at the despondency the thought created. But she couldn't see a way to fight a dead wife's memory. She opened her eyes and took a deep breath of the clean air. Life was what it was; she'd just have to move on and cherish the wonderful things she'd learned from him.

She walked up to the Jernigans' porch and left the basket of blueberry muffins on the table beside the mail slot, knowing Mr. Jernigan would find it when he went to get the newspaper. His elderly wife had been discharged from the hospital yesterday, and everyone knew Mr. Jernigan could burn canned soup.

Back on the sidewalk, Kari trailed after Prince, who knew the route as well as she did. Her sneakers slapped against the pavement, reminding her of the sound of flesh against flesh...of Master Dan plunging into her. *Lordy*. She shook her head, trying to forget that image before she got all heated up again. Impossible task. Too many parts of her ached: her pussy; her swollen mouth; her breasts, almost too sensitive to tolerate her softest bra; her wrists, sore despite the lined cuffs he'd used. She had scrapes on her legs from the straps and a bite mark on her stomach.

Oh, she'd been used and used well. She tried to frown, but her arms wrapped around herself in a do-it-yourself hug, and she laughed instead. Hadn't it just been great?

She danced two steps, then stopped to push little Annie's skates and tricycle off the sidewalk into the grass. Some of those joggers just didn't watch where they were going even in the daylight, let alone at night.

At night...last night, she'd been so aroused that she'd

screamed...actually screamed when she came. So many times too. That was just... Wow.

From across the street, a bird warbled a spring song and received an answer from Debra's yard. For the birds, it was nesting season; for her, it was a time to reexamine her life. She wasn't some frigid, passionless person after all; she just needed something more than other people. Something different. *Exotic*—she'd call it that, since *kinky* didn't sound very respectable.

Seeing Mrs. Jones hadn't retrieved her newspaper, Kari left it on the cushioned chair next to the front door. The frail woman pushed her walker as incompetently as she drove her old Suburban. An accident waiting to happen.

Prince waited for her on the sidewalk and gave her his humans-are-so-slow look before continuing on. Didn't he realize she had thinking to do?

Last night, Master Dan had changed something in her. Her inability to control what happened and his sure knowledge of how far to push her had broken through some barrier she hadn't known was there. She felt like a beginner's chemistry experiment. Add a little sodium bicarb to vinegar and suddenly she bubbled and fizzed with the best of them. Wasn't that just awesome?

Prince trotted back. She stopped to pet him and frowned at the ugly gray sleeve of her sweatshirt. As a new fizzy person, she really should shine up her test tube. She looked down at herself and her baggy gray sweats, then thought about the ankle-length dress lying on the bed for school. Pretty pathetic. Maybe if she didn't dress like an escapee from a nunnery, she would stop thinking of herself that way. Time to go shopping.

On Friday evening, Kari picked up the ringing phone. "Hello."

"Kari, this is Buck."

"Oh. Um. Hi." She sighed. There must be people who enjoyed

going out on Friday evenings, but all she wanted to do was curl up in jammies, eat popcorn, and enjoy a mindless movie. After a week of attempting to teach teenagers, the last thing she wanted was to have a conversation, especially an awkward one. "What's up?"

"We've never had that talk you promised," he said. "How about I come over? We can discuss what's going on."

"Ah, that won't work, Buck. I'm beat." All right, the polite thing would be to say she was sorry, but she wasn't.

A pause. "Are you still mad at me for Monday? I said I was sorry."

Apparently, the discussion would be now. She sat down at the kitchen table and tried to prepare herself. "I'm not mad."

"Well, good. Then I'll pick you up for the last class tomorrow around eight."

Maybe she needed to learn to be less polite. Submissive to one man didn't mean that everyone else could walk all over her. "No. Um. I like you, Buck, but I don't want to date anymore." There. That was plenty blunt. She immediately felt guilty.

"Are you dating that Dom from the club? Is that why you don't want to see me anymore?" His voice held a thread of bitterness.

"I'm sorry, but that's not your business," she said, striving for the gentle-but-firm tone she used with nosy students who wanted to know about her personal life.

"Kari, that guy's not good for you. I can tell," he said. "I don't like the way he's got you behaving."

"I appreciate your concern, but it really is my business." There had to be a way to get off the phone. *Lie*. "Sorry, Buck, but I've got another call coming in. I have to go. Bye."

She punched the End button. Hopefully, he would never remember that she didn't have call waiting. *Bad, bad Kari*.

Saturday evening, Kari set the phone down with a loud sigh. Darn it. No—*damn* it! The auto mechanic had been very apologetic, but the part for her car wouldn't be in until Monday morning. No car till then.

She dropped onto her comfy floral couch and leaned her head back. It wasn't a total disaster. Carol could take her to school on Monday, and she didn't have any place she needed to be this weekend.

Except the Shadowlands.

"Well, Prince, looks like it's you and me tonight."

Setting his head on her knees, the shepherd looked up at her with big brown eyes, perfectly content to have her at home. She stroked his soft ears and sighed. She'd been off and on about returning to the Shadowlands, but now that she couldn't go, she felt a definite letdown. No BDSM stuff. No Master Dan.

Rising, she paced across her living room. She looked at her wrists, remembering the weight of the cuffs and the erotic feeling of helplessness when Sir had strapped her onto that sawhorse thing. How he'd pinned her hips down as he thrust into her, so big and hard... She shivered as her body roused, craving that sensation again. All those sensations.

Still, she needed to be practical. Over the past couple of days, reality had slowly crept back. Although bondage might be interesting, it wasn't exactly something a person did forever...was it?

She reached the end of the room and turned. How long could a person indulge in...*exotic* sex? Hmm. When Jessica had talked about Master Dan being a member of the club, she'd said *years*. And that older couple, Martha and Gerald, had been together for twenty years. They looked perfectly content. Not depraved or anything. So, people *could* do it for years.

Would she want to? Heat ran through her at the thought. What would it be like to be actively interested in sex instead of putting up with it? What if, after an evening of reading or watching TV, her man ordered her to strip and bend over the arm of the couch for his use? Would that change her life? The instant dampness of her pussy gave her the answer.

Master Dan said she was wired to need domination for true satisfaction. A sexual submissive. She wrinkled her nose. That submissive word still sounded awfully distasteful. But facts were facts. She'd gone to the Shadowlands to test the hypothesis that bondage and domination aroused her. Her experiment, although not done to anything resembling scientific standards, had proven exactly that.

Knowledge gained, new problems discovered. Did she want to pursue this further?

She snorted. *Darned right*. Not that she could do anything about it tonight.

Ruffling Prince's fur on the way past, she kept pacing. Couldn't do anything about Master Dan either, now could she? Her introduction to the lifestyle might have been completely different if she'd had a different instructor. Sir was...something. All those muscles to run her hands over, the firmness of his grip on her body, the assured authority. His deep, rough voice. Just thinking of him made her burn.

Would he wonder why she wasn't there tonight? Would he miss her? She shook her head and sighed. Doubtful. With all those subs around, he didn't lack for female attention. Yeah, he wouldn't give her a second thought when she didn't show. Even if she had been able to attend the last class tonight, he'd made it clear their time together was over. The jerk.

He didn't want anything permanent; he wanted his dead wife. So it was just as well that her car was hospitalized. *Really*.

Darn it.

Look on the bright side. By staying home, she wouldn't run into Buck.

Prince whined, reminding her of her petting duties, and she slipped to the floor to hug him. "Buck won't be coming back here again." Prince hadn't liked Buck at all. "I should have listened to you about him, huh?"

In total agreement, Prince licked her face and leaned against her, leaving hair all over her new red tank top and jeans.

She planted a kiss on top of his furry head. "So did you notice? I've got cleavage. And my legs are pretty good too, for that matter." Instead of trying to hide her body, she was finding ways to showcase it and enjoy it. Yesterday, the other teachers had been surprised, then effusive with compliments over her new look. *Thank you, Master.*

"Well, buddy, let me get you some supper and—" Kari stopped. Oh, heck, how could she have forgotten? Jessica expected her to show up early so they could chat. Sir might not miss her, but Jessica would. Kari grabbed the phone again and carried it to her desk. Pulling out a copy of the Shadowlands forms, she found the phone number. Would someone be in the office now?

"Shadowlands." A man's voice. Low. Familiar. One of the DMs?

"Um. This is Kari Wagner. I was supposed to meet Jessica there tonight. Is there any way I can get a message to her?"

"She is here, Kari. Allow me to call her to—"

"No, there's no need. Can you just tell her that I won't be able to make it?"

There was a pause. "Is there a problem, little one? Can I help?"

Her breath caught. This was no DM; it was Master Z. "No. No, really. My car's in the shop, that's all."

"And is your lack of transportation good...or bad?"

The insightful question silenced her. "I..." She sighed. "A little of both, I guess. It's all so different, you know?"

"Kari." His deep voice sharpened. "Did you have a problem with Master Dan?"

Just hearing Sir's name sent blood surging into her face and elsewhere. "No," she managed to say, her words husky. "No, he was—" *Wonderful. Scary. Intimidating. Too much for an inexperienced schoolteacher.* "He was fine."

A chuckle. "I am happy to hear it. I'll give Jessica your message, that you'll be enjoying a quiet evening at home."

"Thank you," Kari said glumly and clicked the phone off. Just hearing a Dom's voice with that edge of command brought back all the reasons she wanted to continue. She yearned to hear Sir tell her what to do, to feel his hands holding her, to struggle and get nowhere.

But he wasn't for her.

She shook her head. *Get over it.* She'd done what she'd set out to do and seen what it was all about. Returning to the Shadowlands would just give her pain, at least until Master Dan had lost some of his appeal. After that, she'd go back and meet someone else.

Until then, maybe she should return to her normal life and normal men. The thought was as appealing as planning to eat oatmeal for three meals a day. Forever. *Darn it.*

Dan drove out of the police station parking garage and turned toward home without any sense of pleasure. His body sagged against the car seat, his mind equally tired. Three hours waiting to be called as a witness, and then the perp settled, a new form to fill out for snitch money. Dan's partner wanted to go on vacation for a month, and who the hell would he end up with then? Some kid fresh from patrol?

Why hadn't he chosen to be an accountant? A quiet office and numbers. No blood, no violence. Far fewer lies. *The paperwork would still suck.*

His cell phone rang, and he pulled off to one side of the freeway. Flipping the phone open, he glanced at the number displayed. The Shadowlands.

"Z? What's up?"

"Not Z, Dan. This is Jessica."

He blinked. Z's sub? "What can I do for you?"

"Well. You know the beginner you were with this week? Kari?"

Knife-edged fear tightened his hand on the phone. "What happened? Is she all right?"

A huff of laughter. "Cops. You always imagine the worst. She's fine. But her car isn't. It's in the shop."

"She called for a ride?" That didn't seem like the little sub. Unlike most women, she didn't beg for release until he tormented her to the point where her brain shut off. Very doubtful that she asked for help often, at least for herself.

"No, you idiot. She called to say she wouldn't be coming. We were planning to meet early, and she wanted me to know."

"Well, that's good she called then." Maybe he'd go tonight then, since she wouldn't be there to mess with his emotions, to lure him into taking more, *giving* more than he wanted.

"Oh." A pause. "Right. It's good. Sorry to have bothered you."

Dan frowned. Had Z's little sub just said "stupid asshole" under her breath?

After pulling back into the heavy traffic, he flipped on the radio, tapping his fingers on the steering wheel to Emmylou Harris. The air off the gulf was briny and warm, the sun setting in a clear blue sky. He'd have time for a shower, maybe a fast bite, before leaving for the club.

She wouldn't be there tonight.

Dan turned the music up louder, ignored the bastard who cut in front of him to make an exit. Tampa drivers terrified the nation: macho Cubans mixing it up with aggressive East Coast drivers tailgating retired snowbirds going twenty miles below the speed limit. Driving was probably the most dangerous part of his job as a cop.

She wouldn't be on the road; she didn't have a car. *She wouldn't be there tonight.*

Good. Very good. He didn't need to see her again. Didn't need any more reminders of her little whimpers right before coming, or the way her hot, soft mouth closed over him, or how her pussy would tighten around him, or—

He slowed to let a bus onto the freeway, breathed in the diesel fumes. The busload of kids was probably headed to a sporting event at the school.

She was a teacher. She'd be a wonderful teacher. He remembered how she'd tried to ease his mind about his carelessness: "*I forgive only if I get a kiss to make it all better, Sir.*" The tender look in her eyes when she kissed him that first night. And—

Fuck. She just wouldn't stay out of his head. He pulled off the freeway, flipped open the phone, and punched in the number.

"Shadowlands." Z's voice. Good thing it wasn't Jessica.

"Give me her damn address, you sadistic bastard."

CHAPTER THIRTEEN

Number thirty-three. Dan pulled into the driveway.

The twilight showed a two-story house, sky blue with sparkling white trim. Bright red and white flowers bloomed along the fence with more in pots on the wide porch. Stepping up to the front door, he rang the doorbell.

When light footsteps sounded from inside, Dan berated himself again. He should stay away from her; she deserved better than what he could give. Dammit, he didn't want anything more from a woman than some mutual satisfaction. Definitely no emotional involvement.

Yet something about her pulled at him. He should never have taken her under command, and he damned well shouldn't be here today. Fuck, he was an idiot.

Hell, she might not even want to see him. He'd behaved like a real asshole on Wednesday. For the second time. What if she didn't want to return to the Shadowlands? Or be with him?

He set a hand against the door frame. Only one way to find out. Any Dom worth his leathers could read a sub's face. He'd soon know if the no-car reason she'd given Z was an excuse.

The door opened, and he had his answer in the big blue eyes.

Surprise, delight, wonder, delight, worry. "What are you doing here?"

He ran a finger down her cheek, unable to keep from touching her. "Jessica said you needed a ride."

"I... You're here to take me to the club? Really?"

"Do you want to go?" He watched her face, her open expressions. She was honest, inside and out. Did she know how rare that was? After years on the force, he'd grown cynical, begun to believe everyone lied. But not this little sub.

"Yes. Mostly." A wrinkle appeared between her brows. "It still doesn't seem real, like something a person should do. But—" She smiled. "Oh, yes, I want to go."

"With me?" He tilted her chin up so she couldn't look away.

The look of longing told him everything he wanted to know even before she whispered, "Yes."

As satisfaction roared through him, he grinned. To hell with his misgivings. He could manage one more night. "In that case, you need to change. Jeans aren't allowed, although..." He ran his gaze down her body. Red top displaying ample cleavage and gorgeous shoulders. Jeans so tight he wanted to bite that sweet ass. "I like what you're wearing."

Her face lit up. "Thanks."

"Definitely my pleasure. I could use a shower if you don't mind. Jessica caught me on my way home, and I detoured here."

"Of course."

"I keep spare leathers in the truck. Let me get those."

A minute later, he walked into her house and stopped short. A German shepherd blocked his path. As a cop, he approved; as the man planning to strip Kari of those jeans, maybe not. He knelt and held out a hand. "Hey, boy."

A thorough sniffing later, he had a new friend. Ruffling the dog's soft fur, Dan said, "He's a beauty. What's his name?"

"Prince."

"Like the musician?"

"Like, someday my prince will come," she said under her breath, adding aloud, "Something like that, yeah. C'mon into the living room."

Cops have keen hearing, and the longing in her words struck Dan like a hard punch to his gut. He froze for a moment until Prince nudged him with a cold nose. "Right, dog. I'm moving."

Escorted by Prince, Dan followed Kari into a living room done in soft pastels, with overstuffed chairs, and a couch in a flowery print. A small white brick fireplace conjured up images of how beautiful Kari would look in the firelight. Tied and helpless and whimpering her need. He shook his head; damn, he was impossible.

"Hello there." A thin woman in her midtwenties rose when he entered the room. Brown hair, brown eyes, maybe five-six.

"Jennifer, this is Mas...um...Dan," Kari said, giving him a flustered look.

He crossed the room, stuck his hand out. "Nice to meet you. I'm sorry for the intrusion."

Jennifer shook his hand. "No intrusion. I'd just come over to ask Kari for some advice on teenagers." She grinned at Kari. "I'll try that and see what happens. Thanks, hon."

She kissed Kari on the cheek and headed for the front door. "You two enjoy yourselves." The door shut quietly behind her.

"Well." Kari glanced at Dan. "My towels are in the dryer. Give me a second."

While she was gone, Dan prowled around. The right side of the living room led to an old-fashioned kitchen with light oak cabinets to match the big round table and chairs at one end. There was a colorful braided rug on the floor, plants in the window over the sink, the scent of cinnamon in the air. Oatmeal cookies were spread on waxed paper. Flour, sugar, and a bottle of vanilla sat on the counter.

She made cookies from scratch? Unable to resist, he took one. Warm and chewy, it brought back memories of weekends at his grandmother's house in the country. Like Kari's home, Gran's place had been cheerful and filled with friends and family. The contrast with his bleak and lonely apartment was chilling.

"Where are—" Towels over her arm, Kari came around the corner into the kitchen. She tried to frown at him, but laughter lit her eyes. "Bad Master! Those are for the children."

"And they're very good." He touched the dimple that appeared in her cheek as she tried not to smile. "You can call me Dan, you know. Formality can be saved for the club. And sex." He smiled as she flushed. "Definitely for sex."

"Well, okay. Thank you." She waved her hand at the counter. "You really can have more, you know. I made plenty. Or can I fix you some supper? Maybe a sandwich?"

A born nurturer. "No. I—" His stomach growled, giving him away.

She laughed and pulled out bread and meats from the refrigerator. "Mustard? Mayonnaise?"

"Just mustard." He leaned against the door frame, watching her bustle about for him. Marion had rarely cooked; she'd assumed he could get his own meals as well as she could. But they—

"What's the matter?" Kari touched his cheek with soft fingers. "You look so unhappy."

"Nothing." No. The cop was taking a cop-out, and a Dom must be honest with himself. And his sub. "I was thinking about my wife. She didn't like to cook."

"Oh." Kari stroked his cheek with light fingers and then returned to making his sandwich. After a minute, she handed him a plate with his sandwich on it, poured a glass of milk, and led him to the big oak table. "Sit. Eat while I put the cookies away."

He'd just finished the sandwich when she joined him at the table and dropped two more cookies on his plate. "You read my mind," he said lightly.

"Men seem to love sweets."

And sweet women like Kari. Damn the way she pulled at him. He shouldn't get involved. Couldn't.

She nibbled on a broken cookie. Then her blue eyes swept up. "Tell me about your wife's death, Dan. How did the accident happen?" she asked softly.

His stomach clenched as the food inside turned to a hard lump. "She skidded off a road into a tree."

Kari tilted her head. Asking more questions would be like deliberately poking at his pain. Horribly rude.

Yet he reminded her of her sister. When Hannah's baby had been stillborn, everyone said she was handling it, only she wouldn't talk to anyone. But Hannah normally shared every little thought or pain. Arriving a week later, Kari prodded until Hannah screamed at her, burst into tears, and finally shared her tangled mess of emotions. More than just grief, Hannah felt guilty over the dumbest things: taking a puff of a cigarette, bouncing too much when she walked, eating something unhealthy. And she'd been envious of every mother with a healthy baby, hated them, hated God, hated her husband, who somehow hadn't prevented the death. Hannah had talked and cried and talked some more.

And after that, she'd been able to simply mourn for the loss of her baby.

Dan's eyes held the same torment. Kari clenched her hands in her lap, her heart aching as she decided to push him. "Were you there?"

His head jerked back as if she'd slapped him.

She waited. "Dan?"

"Dammit!" He slammed his hand on the table so hard the dishes jangled. Pushing to his feet, he stalked across the room. "No. I wasn't there. I got called into work. I could have refused, but I didn't. And she went out partying. Drinking. By herself. If I'd been there..."

"You think if you'd stayed home, she wouldn't have died."

"She'd be alive." At his sides, his hands opened and closed, over and over. The stark lines on his face were deepened by pain. "I protect people; that's my job. And I let my wife die."

A nun once told Kari that guilt has no logic. She kept her voice low the way she did when trying to pet the Garretts' pit bull. "So if I decide not to go tonight, and you get drunk and run off the road, will it be my fault?"

He glared at her, but after years of teaching sneaky little children, she knew how to offer up wide-eyed innocence. "That's not the same at all," he snapped.

"Isn't it?" Kari rose and put her arms around him. His body felt like a stone pillar. "Unless you promised to be at her side every moment of every day, you didn't do anything wrong. People make their own decisions, and sometimes bad things happen. Not your fault, Dan, any more than it would be my fault if you went out tonight and got in an accident."

He didn't move.

Remembering Hannah's anger, Kari added softly, "You know, if you got drunk and killed yourself driving, I'd not only be grieving, I'd be furious with you for doing something so stupid."

He growled, but she ignored that and just held him, her cheek pressed against his chest, feeling his pain, sharing his pain. Had she gone too far? Would he ever talk to her again?

After a minute, he took a ragged breath, and his muscles loosened. Wrapping his arms around her, he held her gently.

She could have nestled there all evening, but the phone rang. He stepped away from her. Feeling like cursing, she went to answer it, after pointing at the table. "Finish your milk."

His huffed laugh relieved her immeasurably.

His legs felt rubbery, as if he'd run a marathon, so Dan took a chair at the table. After a minute, he did as the little sub ordered and drank his milk. The first swallow caught on the tightness in his throat, but the rest went down well enough after that.

Her voice was like a melody of happiness and caring as she talked with some friend about a play rehearsal. Prince padded over to lean against Dan's leg, a comfortingly warm weight. He stroked the soft fur, thinking about Kari's words.

She said she'd be furious if he died being stupid. Was he mad at Marion? He'd loved her, mourned her. But anger?

Now the possibility had been raised, he could almost feel the heavy mass of rage inside him. She *had* been stupid, not for going without him, but in getting drunk and then driving. They'd fought about that before, and she'd laughed at him, called him a hide-bound cop. His jaw tightened. And then she'd died...died and left him alone.

Feeling guilty. Feeling angry.

His eyes burned as the unsettling emotions swept over him, uncontrollable as waves hitting the shore. The room felt suffocatingly hot. He had to leave. He walked out into the night air, leaving Kari staring after him.

Kari heard a tap at her front door and jumped to her feet. *Oh, thank God.* The last half hour had seemed like an eternity. Every few minutes, she'd gone to the door and stood there, wanting to go after him. Then she'd return to the couch and sit down again. After the third time, Prince just stretched out and watched her.

Now she ran to the front door and pulled it open. "Are you all right? I'm so sorry, I should never have said—"

He kissed her firmly. Briefly. "I'm fine, and yes, you should have said everything you did." He ran his finger down her cheek. "I'm sorry I left so abruptly."

"It's all right." She watched him walk into her living room, reassured to see his prowling gait had returned. "Do you still want to go? I'd understand if you didn't."

"Yes, I want to go." He glanced at his watch. "We still have time before Ben locks the doors. Can I take that shower?"

The guest bathroom lacked a shower, so Kari led him down the hall to her bedroom and the master bath. He followed silently —a good thing since she couldn't figure out anything to say. She could talk fine when he'd needed her, but he was back to normal.

And having Master Dan here, in her home, was disconcerting.

Before she'd only seen his Dom side, but there was more to him. The depths of his pain and guilt over his wife's death broke her heart. But it was the little things that she hadn't been prepared for. The way he'd stolen a cookie. How he looked completely at home in her kitchen. How friendly he'd been with Jennifer; he hadn't whipped out cuffs or expected to be called Master. How normal—*gorgeous*—he looked in black jeans and a short-sleeved shirt. How he talked to Prince like a person.

And Prince liked him.

In leathers and at the Shadowlands, Master Dan was like a dream. A fantasy. This Dan was real. Frighteningly real.

"Here you go." She set the towels on the counter.

"Thank you. I'll be quick." He unbuttoned his dark brown shirt and tugged it out of his jeans, before reaching in to turn on the shower.

"Right." Her gaze got trapped at the sight of his muscular chest, his broad shoulders. When he undid his pants, she glanced up and saw the amusement in his eyes. The disconcerting heat that matched her own.

"I'd better change," she muttered and fled.

In the bedroom, she couldn't concentrate. He'd be naked by now. In her shower. If she had any courage, she'd go in there and join him. Yes. She'd do just that. She took two steps toward the door and heard his voice.

"Kari, I need..." The last part of his sentence trailed off.

What could he need? The shower had soap and shampoo. Steam billowed in the bathroom as she entered. Feeling like a voyeur, she hesitated outside the shower curtain, trying not to stare at the outline of his big body. Or at least to not be obvious about it.

"Dan?" Saying his name still felt so strange. Nice, but strange. "Did you need something?"

"I did." He pushed the curtain back, grabbed her around the waist, and set her in the tub. "I need *you*."

The water and his deep laugh drowned out her startled yelp.

With ruthless hands, he stripped her out of her clothes and started washing her, his hands running over her arms, her back, her breasts. He gave extra attention to her breasts. "Cleanliness is next to godliness," he informed her, holding her firmly in place despite her squirming.

"I had a shower earlier." His touch was making her hot, needy. Abandoning modesty, she ran her hands over his chest. "But I guess another one is good." She slid her arms around him and pushed her belly against his erection.

His eyes kindled. "As long as you're there, wash my back." He handed her the soap. Arms around him, she scrubbed his back and butt, each movement rubbing her breasts against his chest. The friction from his chest hair sent tingles running through her.

He took the soap back and returned the favor, although he spent far too long washing her bottom, massaging her cheeks, and running a finger down the crack.

Stepping back, she washed his front, lingering on his chest, searching out the flat nipples and playing with them. His contoured muscles moved under her touch. Where had he been when she'd studied muscle groups in college anatomy? His biceps hardened when he ran his hand up her body; his pectoral muscles flexed when he put his arms around her. Slowly, she worked her way down his front to his—not a penis—he called it his *cock*. The velvety texture seemed incongruous over the iron rod underneath.

She washed his balls, firm and heavy. His legs were apart, his hand stroking her hair as she bent to the task. When she finished and looked up, his eyes were black with passion.

She swallowed hard.

"My turn." He plucked the soap from her motionless fingers. His foam-covered hands slicked over her breasts. When he rolled her nipples between his fingers, her legs weakened. And then he touched her between her legs, sliding over her clit, washing her folds until her knees buckled. He grinned, steadied her, before turning her so her back was toward him.

He removed the flexible shower hose from the overhead clip and dropped it to spray on the tub floor. Taking her hands, he set them low on the shower wall, bending her forward. Her breathing increased.

The curtain slid aside, and a second later, she heard the crinkling sound of a condom wrapper. "Don't move, little sub. I'm going to take you hard and fast," he said. Just his voice sent a shudder through her.

Securing her in place with an iron arm around her waist, he entered her with a hard thrust that raised her up on her toes. She gasped as the shock sent waves of sensation searing through her.

"You feel incredible," he murmured in her ear, one hand caressing her breasts. His chest was hard and hot against her back as he pushed even deeper.

And then he stopped. "Hmm."

Her heart skipped a beat. That sound from him was as ominous as a doctor saying, "Oops."

"Sir?"

He ran a hand down the shower hose and pulled it up. "Seems a shame to waste all this water, doesn't it?"

"What do you mean?" Confused, she glanced at the shower handle. She wiggled her hips a little. He was thick and long inside her; why wasn't he moving? "You can turn it off."

"Oh, no, sweetie, I have a better idea." He twisted the

adjustable head to a single stream. With a hum of satisfaction, he positioned it in front of her breasts. She sucked in a breath at the erotic, brutal sensation.

He moved it down her front slowly, down and down, until the fierce droplets struck her already sensitive clit.

"Master!"

He chuckled, murmured, "Bingo," and held the spray in place, held her in place as he eased his cock out of her. He drove back into her hard, filling her completely. In, out. Each thrust moved her hips forward, changing where the pulsing water struck her clit. Her hips jerked with each assault, her legs trembling so badly, his arm around her waist was all that held her up.

Her clit was on fire, so sensitive that the force of the water throbbed through her whole body. His rhythmic thrusts merged with the sensations, and everything in her tightened. She went onto tiptoes, pushing back against him, needing...needing. He moved the spray suddenly, back and forth, hitting all sides of her clit, and the shock threw her over the peak. Her climax roared over her in a devastating wave, exploding outward as she thrashed in his hard grip.

With a deep laugh, he dropped the showerhead, and grasping her hips in hard hands, he pounded into her, each thrust sending more and more spasms through her. His fingers tightened on her hips and his roar echoed through the small room as he came.

Wrapping his arms around her from behind, he held her through the after-shudders and when her legs went limp. She curled her fingers around his forearms, wanting to hold him tighter. The happiness she'd felt when he climaxed had startled her and worried her a little.

When she could finally stand on her own, he turned her around, kissed her hard on the lips. "There, little sub. Don't you feel better now that you're all clean?"

CHAPTER FOURTEEN

An hour later, Dan walked with Kari up to the front of the club. He stayed far enough behind to enjoy the view of her wearing his shirt...and nothing else. Good thing he carried spare clothing in the truck. He should have guessed that the woman wouldn't own anything a nun wouldn't wear.

He'd considered having her change into the soft cotton pajamas in one drawer, imagining how her breasts would have made SpongeBob dance.

But his hands had ached to play with her butt some more, so he'd put her in one of his spare shirts. The dark blue brought out the color of her eyes and set off her rich brown hair. Even better, the material was thin enough to see each movement of her full breasts. She was so tiny that the shirttail completely covered her ass with a few inches to spare.

Of course, since it was so long, he'd refused to allow her any underwear. Her face had reddened with anger and embarrassment, and her eyes sparked with blue fire. He'd hoped she'd lose her temper, but she remembered her spanking too well... *Dammit.*

He grinned, anticipating his revenge. Sometime tonight, he'd ask her to pick up something from the floor.

She looked back at him, saw where his eyes were focused, and shot him an evil look. "Do you pick out your sub's clothing all the time?"

He closed the gap between them, ran his hand over her bare butt. *God, she was soft*. "No, sweetie, this is just for my pleasure so nothing's in the way when I *take* my pleasure."

Pink washed over the nape of her neck.

At his usual station behind the guard desk, Ben glanced up as they entered. "Kari, good to see you. Jessica hoped you'd make it tonight. Just in time too. I'm closing the doors in a few minutes."

Then he saw Dan, and his mouth dropped open. He glanced at Kari, then Dan again. "I'll be damned."

"Probably so," Dan bit out as the unsettled feeling he'd managed to calm on his long walk reared back up inside him. *Marion. His anger, his guilt, his loss...* All that was bad enough. How he felt about Kari added a different guilt.

And yet he'd wanted to be here with her.

"Well..." Ben rubbed his jaw. "Good. Go on in, folks."

Dan pushed the feelings back down inside him, managed a thin smile. "Thanks, Ben." He nudged Kari toward the inner door.

Kari made it three steps into the club room before she stopped, stunned. Two steps farther than Dan had figured she'd get. The quiet beginners' nights didn't prepare a newbie for a normal Saturday. Tonight, people crowded the small dance floor to the right, dancing to the raw, throbbing music. Across the room, Doms and Dommes, with subs kneeling at their feet, filled couches and tables. The dress code was in force, leather and latex predominant, corsets and loincloths not unusual, the odd disobedient sub wearing only cuffs or collar. They were late enough that the scene areas were in full use, and the slap of a flogger on bare flesh, wails, screams, and moans of arousal sounded over the music.

Kari edged closer to him, looked up with wide eyes, the look on her face so dazed, so innocent, that he had to pull her up against him so he could take her mouth. Damn, but he already wanted her again.

Kari sagged in Master Dan's arms, her body rousing as if she hadn't just gotten off less than an hour ago.

"You're addictive, little sub," he murmured in her ear, biting her neck hard enough to make her shudder with need.

"So are you," she said under her breath. "Dammit." The way he overwhelmed both her body and emotions was frightening.

He frowned, tilted her chin up. "What did you say?"

Oh, spit.

"Kari?"

She huffed a breath. "I said," she muttered. "So are you."

He arched an eyebrow.

"Dammit."

The amusement in his eyes made her want to punch him, but the feeling of his body as he yanked her up against him again wiped the notion out entirely. The warmth of his hands went right through her thin shirt. His leathers brushed her bare thighs, and the feeling of air against her private parts was almost as worrying as the interested looks from everyone walking past. Next time she'd just take the spanking and wear what she wanted.

Or maybe not. She eyed his solidly muscular chest, exposed by the open leather vest, remembered the glint of laughter in his eyes when she'd balked at the no-underwear decree. He'd not only have enjoyed spanking her but would still have stuffed her into his choice of clothing.

The memory of how he'd stripped her clothing off in the shower, pushing her hands away as easily as she'd have brushed away a fly, sent a wave of heat through her and she shivered.

His eyes narrowed. When he rubbed his knuckles against her breasts, she realized her nipples had turned to hard nubs.

"And what are you thinking about, little sub?"

She flushed, didn't answer.

His arm around her tightened. His fingers caught one nipple in a sharp pinch.

When she squeaked, a few people turned to look at them. He didn't even notice.

"Sir!"

"I asked you a question, Kari."

Muffled laughter sounded around them, and she felt her cheeks turning hotter and hotter. "The shower," she whispered. "That's all."

"Ah." He grinned. "Good to know it has such an effect on you." His hand on her butt pressed her against him. He was fully erect. "Thinking about that has the same effect on me. I have a feeling you're going to be a very clean submissive," he whispered in her ear.

She sank against him, loving the feel of his body. Loving the feel of his hands until she realized he'd pulled the tail of the shirt up to her waist so he could touch her bare bottom.

She tried to shove back, but his arm around her waist only tightened. His fingers moved slowly over her buttocks, massaging her cheeks. "Did you forget the rules, sweetling? For tonight, your body is mine to use."

He continued as her outrage passed, as his fingers started to arouse her. The knowledge that people could see made the heat even worse. He tightened his grip, rubbing her against his erection until her pussy throbbed.

"Daniel." Master Z's voice behind her.

Kari stiffened, tried to pull away. Sir's arm didn't loosen, and he held her in place until she stopped pushing. Finally, finally, his point made, he released her.

She turned and looked up at Master Z, her face probably as red as a tomato. To her surprise, he had his arm around Jessica. Was Jessica his sub?

"I'm so glad you made it here." Jessica frowned as her gaze

swept over Kari. She shook her head at Master Dan. "I wanted you to give Kari a ride, not to ride her."

Sir barked a laugh, then said, "Z, your sub's getting mouthy. Called me an asshole earlier."

Master Z tilted his head. "Did she now? If she sets such a bad example for our beginners, she will need to demonstrate what follows." He paused, said reflectively, "I haven't given a lesson on discipline for some time."

Jessica froze, her eyes widening. A tremor shook her body.

Smiling slowly, Master Z looked down at Jessica and murmured, "Thank you for the suggestion, Daniel."

Chuckling, Sir pulled Kari away.

Kari rose up on tiptoe to whisper, "What did he mean by 'demonstrate' and 'a lesson'?"

"Master Z teaches by demonstrating how something should be done."

Discipline? Oh God, poor Jessica.

Moving through the crowd, Sir kept a hard arm around Kari, and she loved how feminine and protected his strength made her feel. When they reached the bar, she snuggled even closer.

He glanced at her and ran a finger down her cheek. "I like touching you, little sub," he said, his eyes gentle.

Her breath seemed to stop inside her chest.

But then he grinned and his hand trailed to where the shirt gaped open over her breasts. His voice lowered. "And I also like spanking your ass until it's a glowing red. And fucking you hard against a wall."

She put her fingers over his mouth to silence him, but his amused look said he knew how his carnal words sent hunger through her and wet seeping between her legs.

Cullen wandered over and set drinks in front of them. His gaze lingered on her heated face. "A sub for three nights, Dan. That's gotta be a record."

She felt Sir's body stiffen against her as his muscles turned iron hard. "Don't jump to conclusions," he growled. "I'm just helping out with beginners' nights like I promised Z. Nothing else." His arm dropped.

His words sucked the air right out of Kari's chest.

Again. Nothing had changed. She turned her face away, her gaze coming to rest on Martha and Gerald across the bar. The old Dom nuzzled his wife, the caring so obvious in his actions that Kari's lips tightened. Their affection made her realize she'd hoped for that with Dan. Especially after he'd come to get her, and they'd shared so much.

Well, obviously that wasn't going to happen. How could she keep forgetting he didn't want anything more than an occasional fucking? She deliberately used the *f* word, squeezing her hands together so hard the joints ached.

How had she been so delusional? This place wasn't about love; it was about domination. Pain. Sex. She'd been stupid.

"The sub you're with tonight isn't adequately dressed." Cullen's lazy tone had turned mean. Was he mad at her or at Sir?

Master Dan glanced at her, his gaze shuttered. "Very true. Got a spare set of cuffs?"

Cullen crossed the bar, opened a cupboard, and returned to thump down leather cuffs.

"Give me your wrists, Kari," Sir snapped.

She hesitated. Did she even want to be with him tonight? How much of this high and low stuff could she take? Then again, she was just here for the sex. Just the sex. Nothing more.

Mouth tight, she slapped her wrists into his broad hand, ignoring his narrowed eyes.

He buckled the cuffs on, checked for the tightness automatically, his gaze not leaving her face.

She looked away. *Just the sex, nothing more.*

"Interesting attire, Dan," Raoul said, sliding onto the bar stool next to where Kari stood. He nodded at the shirt she wore. "Amazingly provocative on her."

"I like it," Sir said. He didn't snap at Raoul, she noticed. "She wasn't happy."

"Like anyone would be." Kari yanked the bottom of the shirt lower and scowled. Damn him anyway. She should have just stayed home. "You can see right through it, and it hardly covers my—"

Raoul raised his eyebrows, and Kari's breath strangled in her throat. *Oh dear Lord.* Holding her lip between her teeth, she ventured a look at Master Dan and tried not to cringe at the expression on his face. This wasn't the hurt man whom she'd hugged in her living room. This was Master Dan, and her fantasy of him had just taken on a nightmarish tinge.

His gaze chilled her right to the bone. "Apparently your modesty weighs more heavily with you than my will. Rather surprising you have any modesty left, considering how you spent a good portion of Wednesday night." He glanced up at the chains on the rafters.

"I'm sorry, Master. Very sorry." She lowered her eyes, heart hammering in her chest. Would kneeling help?

"I am sure you are," he said quietly and started unbuttoning her shirt. Her hands rose instinctively to stop him. His hard look made her drop her arms back to her sides. "Toss me a towel, Cullen," he said.

He used the towel to cover a bar stool, lifted her onto it, and flipped the shirt open. With unyielding hands, he moved her legs apart until her private parts showed, her brown curls blatantly dark against the white material.

"Please, Master," she whispered.

"Please is the right word, sub," he said. "And that's what you'll do. Please both yourself and me." He took her hands, placed them over her breasts. "Play with your breasts until your nipples are as swollen and red as I had them three days ago."

She shook her head.

"What do you say to me?"

Her fingers flinched as he moved her hands, massaging her

breasts, ruthlessly plucking her nipples until fire streaked toward her groin. "Yes, Sir," she said, unable to look away from his lethal brown eyes.

He stepped away. She tried to move her hands like he wanted and ended up covering her breasts with them instead.

His jaw clenched. "Kari, do what I said, or I'll lay you out on the bar and use my mouth to do it myself."

Even as she recoiled, heat flooded her insides, and the towel dampened under her. Sir's lips curved up mockingly, even though his eyes remained frozen.

Gritting her teeth, she touched her breasts, stroking, pulling on the nipples, pinching them. Club members stopped to watch with appreciative looks before smiling at Master Dan. Eyes half-lidded, Cullen propped an elbow on the bar, acting like he was at a movie. Kari raised her chin and looked away.

When Master Dan turned his back on her, she continued, her hands trembling as embarrassment seared her again and again with each laugh and half-heard comment. Buck—oh, God, Buck—started to approach, then stopped. He shot Dan a nasty look and moved away.

When Master Dan finally checked on her, he frowned. Nudging her hand away, he took a nipple between his fingers, pinching and rolling with increasing force until pain, then pleasure, shot through her, hammering into her clit. Her breath sucked in.

"That hard," he said coldly. "Last warning, sub."

She nodded miserably. Closing her eyes to shut out the world, she touched herself. Harder, faster. To her shock, her body roused; her pussy ached as her breasts swelled and tightened. Her nipples moved past sensitive to throbbing need.

Hands closed on her wrists, held her immobile. She opened her eyes. "Master?"

"You can stop now, Kari."

Her hands fell to her sides, shaking. Her lips quivered.

He studied her, and the hardness eased from his face. His brown eyes warmed. He rubbed his knuckles over her jutting nipples, and she sucked in an audible breath at the gentle abrasion. "Now that's a very pretty color," he said. His smile sent pleasure through her, melting the lump in her chest and almost making her forget why she'd been so mad at him.

He tilted her chin up to pin her with his gaze. "Whose body is this tonight, sub?"

"Yours, Master."

"If this body is mine and I want to show it off, should you be embarrassed?"

"No, Sir."

He nodded. "Good enough for now. You did well." After buttoning her shirt, he cupped her cheek so gently that her eyes puddled with tears. "Kari, I should let you go. I know that, and you know that. You deserve a Dom who can give you more than a night here and there."

If she'd been standing, she would have fallen. Instead, she firmed her spine and curled a hand around his wrist, resting her fingertips on the hard tendons. "I'm here tonight for the sex. Nothing more."

He could undoubtedly read the lie in her face, but he didn't challenge her. "So be it." He turned her bar stool to face the bar and tucked an arm around her waist.

The warmth of his touch made her tremble inside fully as much as she shook outside.

Cullen appeared, removed her untouched, watery drink, and set a fresh one down.

Master Dan handed it to her and asked Cullen, "Anything interesting happening tonight?"

"Looks to be a good night. Raoul plans to scene with his sub. Flogging, I think, then the cane. Mistress Anne brought in some new toys and was going to demo them on her sub later. Cock cage, ball crushers."

"Anne is usually a good show."

"True." Cullen's fingers tapped the bar as he thought. "Ah, Z's opening the Capture Gardens. Said he'd save you a spot."

"Well, now." The change in Master Dan's voice whipped Kari's head around. Anticipation and amusement. One side of his mouth curved up as he looked at her. She knew that expression, and it made her insides quake.

"In that case, give me another set of cuffs, small plug, and lube," Sir said. "And what time?"

"Anytime now." Cullen looked at Kari, his eyes filled with the same amusement as Sir's. "Kari. You may want another drink."

Kari choked on the sip she'd just taken.

CHAPTER FIFTEEN

The jerk hadn't bothered to explain anything. Fuming, Kari had barely finished her first drink when three chimes sounded over the music. Heads lifted all through the room.

"Wha—" She closed her mouth quickly, earning herself a frown from Sir, but nothing more.

"The Gardens are open." He led her to an open door on the right wall and into a room with a stone floor and darkly paneled walls. About twenty members congregated there. On the far side, a door leading outside stood open. The scent of night-blooming jasmine and newly cut grass wafted in.

An older DM, one of those who'd touched Kari's breasts on Wednesday, faced the crowd. His light blue eyes met Kari's, and he winked.

She flushed, then wondered if she'd ever lose that response. Probably not. Really, modesty should have been her middle name.

"My name is Sam," the DM said. "I'll be your contact for any problems during this role-play. There are rules, and as Master Z has decided upon the punishments, you want to listen closely. He can be a sadistic bastard." A ripple of laughter ran through the crowd.

"For those who haven't participated before, the game is this. Your sub is released into the Garden with a head start. You search for her or him," he added, nodding at a gay couple and a Domme with a male sub. "Once found, take whatever satisfaction you and your sub have agreed upon, either right in the Gardens, inside on the equipment, or upstairs in private."

Kari's eyes widened. On the first night, Sir had asked her about her fantasies. "*A gorgeous barbarian taking you against your will? Have you had that one*?" Her insides quivered. Was this real?

Sir leaned over to whisper, "When I catch you, I will take you right then and there." His hand slid over her bare butt, squeezing possessively.

She bit her lip against the surge of arousal.

Sam continued, "Resistance is expected, but serious fighting is forbidden; no deep scratching, punching, or hard kicking for either subs or Doms. Subs, the club safe word is red, and DMs will be in the Gardens."

"Doms, you may only capture the sub whose band matches yours." Motioning the gay couple forward, Sam fastened bright green glow-sticks around the Dom's wrist and matching ones on his sub's ankle and wrist. "Chasing anyone else's sub is forbidden. Of course, if one blunders right into you, feel free to cop a feel and then swat her to get her running again. Anything more than that..." Sam's smile was pure evil. "Well, the last Dom who tried for more was flogged by Mistress Rachel until her arm wore out, and then his membership was canceled. Pissing off Z isn't smart.

"The game lasts two hours, and three chimes mean the game is over. Subs, a few idiots have managed to hide by removing their glow-sticks. This is your warning. At closing, the DMs search the Gardens. Any sub still outside is considered available for use by any and all DMs who join the search."

. . .

As Sam finished his lecture, Dan realized Kari had pressed so closely to his side, she almost melted into his skin.

She looked up at him with big eyes. "I don't think I want to do this."

So modest and so passionate. Why did the discrepancy bring all his Dom urges to the forefront? He rubbed his cheek against her silky hair and whispered back, "I know you really do want to. I can see...smell your arousal."

Her eyes widened, probably from his language. And then, brave little sub, she nodded.

The line moved forward as Z vetted the players; mind games like this brought out his overprotective nature. Now Z shook his head at the couple in front of them. "Sorry, Adam, but Beth isn't ready for this yet. She's terrified."

"But—" Adam scowled and shrugged. The bunched muscles in Beth's bared shoulders eased as she and her top for the night stepped out of line.

Dan smiled at the slender redhead and received a fleeting smile in return. He'd once considered topping her before realizing she only chose weaker Doms. Sub or not, she wasn't about to give up much control. Something nasty must have happened in her past to make her so wary.

He and Kari stepped up to face Z.

"Little one, do you understand how the game works?" Z studied Kari. "You'll be running away from Master Dan. When he catches you, he gets to do whatever he wants."

Kari shivered, then nodded.

Z glanced at Dan. "She has a nice mixture of fear and anticipation." Smiling, Z nodded to Sam, who fastened a bright pink glowstick around both their wrists and another around Kari's ankle.

"Pink, huh." Dan shook his head at Sam. "Thanks a lot, you bastard."

"But you're so *pretty* in pink, Master Dan."

Fighting was forbidden in the club, so Dan just thumped Sam on the chest on the way past. Sam barked a laugh.

Once clear of the line, Kari tugged on Dan's arm. He leaned down to hear her whisper, "But you *do* look pretty in pink, Master."

"Just keep it up, sub, just keep it up," he warned.

When she giggled, his brain went stone-cold dead. He'd never heard her laugh, not like that. He grinned, wanting more. He needed to... No, he didn't need anything. No more evenings, dammit.

They walked a few more paces while he subdued his emotions.

"Master?"

He nodded permission for her to speak.

"I run, and you catch me. I understand that. But I'm not much of a runner, you know."

Dan tipped Kari's face up. "I enjoy a good chase, so I'll add an incentive. If you don't try hard—say, if I catch you within fifteen minutes—then I'll show you how the spanking bench works in the bar room. Do you understand?"

If her blue eyes got any bigger, they'd take over her whole face. "Yes, Master."

He could hardly wait to get his hands on her. "I'll even be nice and give you a fighting chance." He removed her cuffs.

"Dan." Nolan strolled over.

Damn, it was good to have him back. "We got fog tonight?"

Nolan nodded. "Z went all out. There's dry ice in every fountain."

Dan smiled at Kari's puzzled expression. She'd understand soon enough. "You doing the subbie preps?"

"My favorite job, especially since returning. You wouldn't believe how overdressed women are in Iraq." Nolan nodded at Kari. "Clothing? Oil?"

Dan studied the little sub. Her eyes were wary but bright, her breathing fast. Not too scared. He could have her prepped in his favorite way. "No clothes, lots of oil."

"Well, now, that will be my pleasure." Nolan turned to Kari, his faint smile fading. "Sub, hang your shirt on the hook over there and return to me to be prepared."

Her eyes whipped up to Dan's.

"Kari, go with Master Nolan."

"But..."

Nolan scowled, his voice cruel. "What do you say to me, sub?"

She flinched and gave Dan a look of betrayal before dropping her eyes. "Yes, Master." She unbuttoned the shirt and pulled it off slowly.

Nolan smothered a grin as Dan's sub hung her shirt on a hook and tried to act nonchalant. She looked around, obviously hoping no one saw her. Of course, everyone did. Grins appeared on the other Doms' faces; even Master Z's lips curved up before he turned to the next couple.

Nolan remembered this little one from last Wednesday. No man with a dick would forget those lush and responsive breasts. Considering Dan's preference for voluptuous and sweet, Nolan figured the Dom might end up keeping this sub. A good thing. He'd been alone too long.

Nolan stomped on the envy rising within him.

As Kari approached, he looked her over slowly. Coldly. Part of prep included increasing a sub's anxiety, and with his scarred face, he was damned good at it. Odd how a man could enjoy scaring a sub and simultaneously want to cuddle her up and reassure her. Just one of those oddities of being a Dom.

He set a hand on her curvy ass just to feel her recoil and pushed her outside. The night air was warm and humid, perfect for playing in the Gardens.

Behind them, a sub in a lacy corset and tight latex pants let out a high shriek, then darted out the door and into the Gardens. Nolan glanced down at Kari. She chewed on her lip, obviously dying to ask why that sub got to keep her clothes and she didn't. Dan had trained her a bit, since she managed to keep silent.

A few feet to the right of the door, another DM, Jake, leaned against the wall, a sprayer at his feet. The DM's appreciative gaze ran over Kari. "Who's this?"

"Dan's sub."

"Oh, yeah, a newbie. I saw her on Monday. Very cute." Jake gave her another approving look, then straightened. "Don't move, *chica*."

Nolan stepped back as Kari froze in place like a terrified rabbit. After pumping up the sprayer, Jake opened up. She flinched as the fragrant oil hit her, covering her shoulders, above her breasts, across her back, drizzling down her skin.

After one complete circle, Jake stepped back. "Been thinking. We should change jobs."

"Nope." Seniority had its rewards. Nolan stepped forward and closed his hands on the sub's soft shoulders.

"No!" She jerked back and put her hands up.

Damn, but the shy ones were fun. Nolan growled, "Stand very still, subbie, or I will chain you to the door and let everyone have a turn. Or do you want to use your safe word?"

Even with the patchy moonlight, he saw her face pale, but she shook her head. Mouth pressed into a tight little line, she lowered her hands.

Taking his time, he stroked the oil over her body, down her arms, her hands, her shoulders, and back, enjoying the satiny skin and curves under his hands. No wonder Dan liked her.

"Spread your legs, sub." Her hands fisted, but she complied. Kneeling, he spread oil over her legs, smoothing down and then back up. A pity he couldn't do her cunt too, but oil wasn't good for pussies. When he stopped at her upper thighs, her tiny exhale of relief made him grin.

He heard Jake chuckle.

Unfortunately for her, he wasn't done yet. Rising, he gripped her upper arm to secure her—the little rabbit looked ready to scamper—and massaged the oil into her breasts, taking his time. His father always said, "*If a job is worth doing, it's worth doing well.*"

He'd seen Dan force her to play with herself earlier and figured she'd be pretty sensitive now. And yes, her breasts swelled all too quickly under his hands. *Damned shame*. So he concentrated on her nipples until her muffled whimpers became audible. Until pink arousal showed in her cheeks.

He rubbed the back of his hand over the brown curls of her pussy. Very, very wet. She closed her eyes in humiliation. Well then, his job here was done. "Sub."

Her eyes opened, and a tremor ran through her as she stared up at him with huge blue eyes.

"Looks like you're ready to give Master Dan a good time. Off with you now." He pushed her toward the Gardens and smacked her bare bottom hard enough to make her yelp.

She ran. Once past the first tall hedge, fog appeared, pooling on the grass, curling upward like white fingers, giving the area a surreal atmosphere. Slowing, she moved past curving flower beds, heady with fragrance. Tall bushes and trees formed secluded nooks.

In the eerie mist, small fountains glimmered with soft lights, the only illumination in the gardens other than faint moonlight and the glow-sticks that darted here and there like colorful lightning bugs.

Okay. She needed to evade Master Dan for at least fifteen minutes, but how could anyone hide in here? The bushes were too thick to burrow into, the fountains too small to hide behind. Swings and flat lawn chairs offered no shelter. Even the soft grass was cut golf course short.

And look how the other subs' light sticks danced. Way too visible.

Suddenly a man's voice rose. "Masters, the chase is on. Find your slaves and make them pay for trying to escape."

Kari shivered. This might be just a game, but knowing Sir hunted her, planned to take her, made her insides feel funny. Scared. *Aroused.*

Spotting a pink glow that matched her bracelet, she ran across an open space and dodged behind more bushes. She stopped next to a gurgling fountain and saw white mist boiling from the water, spilling over the concrete sides like a volcano erupting. The fog suddenly turned silver, and Kari glanced up. Slow-moving clouds revealed the moon before hiding it again, darkening the world.

A sub ran past, her master in full chase. A squeak like a captured rabbit sounded a minute later, then high-pitched begging. Slaps of a hand hitting flesh and cries of pain.

Kari put a hand over her mouth. The sub hadn't yelled out a safe word, so she didn't need help. Did she?

Hands behind his back, a DM strolled toward her, obviously listening for trouble. Kari relaxed slightly.

He spotted her. His gaze ran over her, lingered on her breasts, and stopped on her bracelet. With a grin, he pointed to the left. Kari saw a pink glow heading closer, and she gasped.

"Run, subbie," the DM said, amusement in his voice, and waved her off.

Breasts bouncing, she ran, weaving through the clearings, trying to find a barrier to block the glow-stick light. She ran some more. Had it had been fifteen minutes? She turned a corner and froze at the sight of a pink bracelet moving across a clearing. Master Dan. His shadow reached toward her like a monster from underground, the cuffs clipped to his leathers rattling.

What if she hadn't used up all the time?

Struggling for breath, she fled, sprinting past more fountains, veering one way, then another. Past a man pounding into a woman on all fours, past a man with arms chained to a low branch.

A hand grabbed her wrist. She squeaked, yanked, and Sir's fingers slid off her oil-covered arm. She dashed away, but he seized her within a minute and again lost his hold.

A couple of yards farther, his body thudded into hers from behind, and his arms wrapped around her waist, securing her.

She struggled, trying to push his hands away. No success. Then she lifted her feet and dropped, sliding right out of his arms. She rolled, pushed to her knees.

With a laugh, he flattened her under his heavy body, knocking the wind out of her. "Sneaky little sub."

With forceful hands, he flipped her onto her back. She started fighting again, instinctively trying to escape the hard hands holding her in place. His grip slipped, and he cursed, then straddled her, pinning her to the ground with his weight. Using his knee, he trapped one arm long enough to buckle a wrist cuff on. He did the other wrist and secured the cuffs together in front. He sat back on his haunches.

"Sweetheart, you're faster than a rabbit." His eyes heated. "And very slick." His hands stroked down her neck and her shoulder.

Holding her cuffs over her head with one hand, he kissed her hard, taking her mouth slowly. Thoroughly. His fingers played with her breasts, erotically slipping and sliding over her oily skin, toying with her nipples until her hunger grew overwhelming. When her hips tilted up toward him, he sat back and grinned wickedly.

The look in his eyes boded ill for her comfort level. What was he thinking? She glanced around the small, way-too-open clearing where fog drifted in small patches of white. No equipment, no benches, or crosses. *Good. That was good.*

When he rose to his feet, she made her move, rolling over and away. He snatched an ankle before she could rise and then wrapped a cuff around it. The other ankle got a cuff too.

She squirmed harder, and he chuckled. "Fight all you want, little sub. You're doomed." Pulling her to her feet by the wrist cuffs, he led her across the clearing to a picturesque grouping of three trees. Trees, wrist cuffs—this didn't look good.

"This looks good," he murmured. "Kneel."

"Sir," she whispered, bracing her feet. "There are people here."

"How about that?" he whispered back. Grabbing her around the waist, he laid her flat and threw a leg over her to keep her in place. She pushed at him. Got nowhere.

"Put your hands over your head."

Was he insane? "No." She shook her head frantically. "Not here."

He sighed and rolled her onto her side, pinning her legs between his own, and smacked her bottom, a hard, stinging blow. She barely managed to muffle her yelp.

"Put your hands over your head, Kari." His hand stroked over her burning skin. "Or don't. I would enjoy spanking you first."

He would too.

When he pushed her onto her back, she lifted her hands over her head, horrified at how vulnerable she felt. Outside. In public.

And yet, when he snapped the cuffs to a chain wrapped around the base of the tree, her breasts tightened and she dampened. As he rose to his feet, a quiver of panic went through her. Why had he put ankle cuffs on her? She looked around and realized chains circled the tree trunks with the ends dangling.

He grabbed her right ankle, lifting her leg into the air and snapping it to a chain that was waist high on the tree.

"No, Master. No." She kicked at his hands. He laughed, snatched her other foot, and secured her left ankle to a chain on the other tree. Her legs now formed a narrow V in the air.

He rubbed his cheek and studied her. "Wider would be good." Shortening the chain on the left tree, he reclipped her ankle cuff, pulling her legs farther apart. The misty air that struck her wet labia was as shocking as ice.

"I love being outdoors, don't you?" he said in a normal voice, kneeling between her legs.

"Shhh," she whispered. "There are people around."

"We're in the shadows. Mostly." Then he chuckled, traced a finger through her wet folds, making her squirm. "However, if I'm any good at all, the entire garden will hear you scream when you come."

Oh God. "I don't want to do this," she hissed, glaring at him.

CHAPTER SIXTEEN

Dan tried to smother his laugh. She couldn't get much wetter or more aroused. "Poor Kari. I can tell you're turned off by the whole thing." His finger circled her clit, and she wiggled like a worm on a hook. "You're lying to me, sweetheart. Have we talked about honesty?"

Her eyes widened.

Lying down on top of her, he braced himself on one forearm. Her soft breasts cushioned his chest; her soft thighs cradled his hips.

Grasping her chin roughly, he frowned down at her. "How many times did you tell me no in the last five minutes? And now you're lying. You're racking up the punishments you have coming. I'd suggest you confine yourself to 'yes, Sir' before I decide to make some of them very, very public."

Those big eyes. He could never describe the way they pulled at him, the satisfaction he got from seeing the nerves revving in them, the wariness, and the trust when she let him drive her to the heights. He took her mouth hard, pulling a response from her. When he squeezed her breast, he felt her nipple's hard point of arousal. Her trembling increased.

There was nothing more gratifying than a sub's sweet yielding.

Or a sub's squirming when being punished. He pushed back onto his knees, kneeling where he could see her pussy, a dark triangle in the misty shadows. Pulling the toy, lube, and condom from his pocket, he opened his leathers and sheathed himself. With the lube, he prepared the plug. "You might find this a bit different, little sub, but I think you'll like it...eventually."

He was holding something the length of her finger, shaped like a rocket with a flat base. It glistened with lubricant, and now he ran his hand down her thighs to her bottom. He spread her cheeks apart. When his fingers touched her rectum, a horrifying realization hit.

"No! Don't." She jerked at the restraints futilely.

A second later, something slid into her rectum, hard and cold, sending shivers through her at the sheer unfamiliarity of it.

"Take it out!" she whispered, moving her hips, trying to escape.

"No."

She gasped as he plunged a finger into her vagina, moving it against the swollen, sensitive walls. He lowered himself in the grass. His hair brushed her inner thighs, and his hot breath skimmed over her folds.

"Master." Her voice cracked. "Please."

"Try the plug this once, Kari, and we'll talk about it afterward." He touched the thing again, making it move inside her, and she gritted her teeth at the raw, carnal feeling. His fingers moved and then it started to vibrate inside her, an almost soundless buzz that set unfamiliar nerves to firing. Her hips lifted off the ground as waves of increasing pleasure ran through her from the unfamiliar direction.

And then his fingers pulled back her folds, opening her farther, exposing her engorged clit. He licked up and over the nub, and she bucked in his grip at the feeling of his hot, wet tongue. She almost climaxed right then.

He pulled back. "Not yet." Waited as her body ached for him.

Finally, he lowered his head again. The thing in her vibrated away as his tongue slid and flicked over her clit.

She panted, shot back into hard arousal.

When he slid a finger up inside her, she moaned at the exquisite sensation. He added another finger, moving slowly in and out, circling the walls of her vagina. The thickness of his fingers pressed the walls against the anal plug, sending vibrations coursing through all of her, until every nerve between her thighs pulsed intensely.

Her thighs, her stomach, her whole body tightened as he played with her. She sucked in a sobbing breath. She was close, so close—

His tongue moved away from her clit, his fingers stopped. "No, you don't have permission to come."

She moaned. "Please, Master."

He didn't answer. When her breathing slowed, he started again, brought her up and up...and stopped.

Her head rolled back and forth, her hips raised to him. She whined as everything inside her throbbed.

After a minute, he restarted and ruthlessly teased her until her clit was on the excruciating edge of climax and her need was so great that the world narrowed to each touch of his mouth, his fingers.

He lifted his head and removed his fingers from inside her.

"Oh, no, please..." Her legs shook as she sobbed for release, her voice rising uncontrollably. "Please, Master. Oh, please, please, please."

Chuckling, he pushed himself up and, a second later, plunged his cock deep inside her, impaling her so hard that she screamed at the exquisite feeling. Her tissues were so swollen, so sensitive, that each slide of his shaft increased the storm of sensation assailing her. His thick cock pressed against the vibrating thing in her bottom, and her body shuddered.

The feelings grew overwhelming, and she stiffened, every muscle tightening as she hung on the precipice. Even her breathing stopped.

"Come now, Kari. Come," he ordered in a deep voice. His hard fingers pinched her jutting clit, and her world went white. She screamed, screamed again as he thrust in and out of her, her mind in splinters and her vagina convulsing around him.

An eternity later, she blinked up at him, her body still giving little shudders. His corded arms planted beside her shoulders, and his eyes dark with passion, he waited, unmoving.

Her legs were still in the air, her arms over her head. "Let me free," she demanded, her voice husky.

His lips curved in a smile. "Little sub, you're going to regret being so bossy," he murmured. Ignoring her demand, he pinned her hips with one hard hand so he could pound into her even deeper and harder. The steady rhythm took her past her climax and started building another. As arousal flared in her, she tried to lift her hips to meet his, but his hand held her just where he wanted her. His thumb slid in circles over her clit.

She whimpered at the building need, at the sensations shooting through her.

He was merciless, his cock massive. Her hips jerked uncontrollably within his grip; her trembling legs made the chains chime. Each plunge of his shaft, each sweep of his thumb over her sensitive clit sent her further out of control.

"Sir?" Unable to think, only to feel. "I can't—"

"Come again, Kari. Come now." His thumb pressed down as he thrust deeply into her, and she exploded, feeling her blood boiling from her pelvis to her fingertips. Short screams escaped her as she shook like a breaking doll in his grip.

His fingers tightened, and his cock drove deep, reaching far up inside her. He groaned as his release jerked inside her, making her buck and shiver.

She roused a minute later. He pulled out, leaving her hollow, and then removed the thing inside her. When he stood and moved away, she shot awake. "Master!"

"Easy, sweetheart, I'm right here." He returned from across the clearing. His hands were gentle as he released her restraints, lowered her legs. She groaned as her joints and muscles protested.

Lying down beside her on the soft grass, he pulled her into his arms, the embrace so comforting, so welcome, that her breath shuddered. She'd dropped every barrier she had under his hands, his body. He'd seen her at her most vulnerable, and when he held her like this, she felt closer to him than she had to anyone before.

He tucked her head into the hollow of his shoulder. One arm kept her close while his hand stroked her hair, her arm, her side, and the tenderness of his touch, the care he took with her, made her heart swell.

After a minute, she remembered where they were. She was naked; her legs had been in the air. Everyone in the whole county had probably heard her screaming her release. *Oh, God.*

"Now what was that thought?" he asked. In the wavering light from the fountain, she could see his dark eyes crinkling in a smile.

"I was...loud."

He laughed, deep and satisfied. "You certainly were. You know, you sound different when you get off." He kissed the top of her head.

"How so?"

"You normally have a soft voice. Careful and polite." His finger circled her breast, teased the nipple until it budded. "But when you climax, your voice is raw. Carnal. Nothing held back." His pleasure was obvious.

She groaned and hid her face against his chest. *She could never face any of those people again.*

He rubbed his chin on the top of her head and chuckled.

As she breathed in, his scent surrounded her, mixed with the fragrance of oil on her body and their lovemaking. Sighing, she hitched an arm over his chest and pulled him closer. "I wish we could just lie here and never leave," she murmured.

She knew the words were a mistake the minute they left her mouth.

His muscles stiffened, and his arm around her loosened. She closed her eyes as grief hollowed her chest. Withdrawing again? How could he keep doing this to her?

"Kari." He sat up, pulling her with him. His hand cupped her chin. Even in the dim light, she could see his face had that...that *damned* cold look again. "Don't get attached to me. It can't—"

The lovemaking and then his tender attention had lowered the shield she'd put over her heart, and now his coldness stabbed into her chest. The anger she'd bottled up surged out of control. She slapped his hand away from her face. "Can't, don't, mustn't."

A muscle in his jaw tightened.

She shoved to her feet and glared down at him.

"You big jerk. You tell me there should be honesty between a Dom and his sub. It goes both ways, you know." Her voice rose to a shout; she couldn't control it any more than she could her temper. "There's more between us than just sex, and you *know* it. But you're afraid of me. You're afraid to live."

She unbuckled her ankle cuffs and dropped them onto the ground. He sat silently, watching her with unreadable eyes, his jaw tight. Rage swelled inside her until she choked with it. She fumbled with the wrist cuffs. They came off finally, and she threw them at him, watched them bounce off his unmoving chest.

"Damn you." She choked on the words, the pain growing inside her. "I d-deserve more than this. I'm going to find someone who will appreciate me."

Silence.

Furious, she sliced at him one last time. "You know, you're not mourning her anymore; you're just too scared to move on."

Hand over her mouth, trying to keep the sobs inside, she ran from the clearing. Ran until she discovered a fence at the far end of the Gardens. Wrapping her arms around herself, she slumped against the rough wood. Tears slid down her face onto her bare breasts as the angry fire inside of her faded, then died, leaving only ashes behind. She wanted to go home, home where her life was safe and normal, where Prince loved her.

Finally, she took a shuddering breath and shook her head. She was whining like a child not getting something. *Someone*.

God, how pitiful. She pushed off the fence. Walking through the mist-filled Gardens, she caught glimpses of others, flashes of bare skin, eyes watching her. The whole place had probably heard her yelling. She didn't care. Didn't care about this place, this lifestyle, or about him either. Especially not about him. He was so stupid, so dumb, so cowardly, and she...

Wanted him. Damn him. How had she gotten so...attached... as he called it, despite all his warnings?

But she had. And he didn't return the sentiment. *Fine*. She wanted to spit at the bitter taste in her mouth. Spit at him. She'd find someone who did want her. There must be other clubs in Tampa.

But the thought of someone else touching her made her—

"Kari." Dan's deep voice came from across the secluded glade. He stepped out of the shadows, the moonlight carving shadows across his muscular chest. "You're right, sweetheart. I didn't—"

Growling like an animal, someone slammed into him, knocking him against a tree. Kari heard the *thud* of his head against the trunk. He dropped, stunned.

She started to run to him, then stopped. The attacker was tall. Blond hair glinted in the moonlight. "Buck?" Kari whispered.

"You leave her alone, you bastard," Buck yelled. Straddling Dan, he punched him in the face.

"No!" Kari yelled, running across the clearing. She kicked Buck in the back of his head, her bare foot bouncing off his skull.

He turned. "Kari, honey. I heard you yelling. I'll—"

Dan hit him hard, knocking him completely over. And then Dan was on his feet, legs spread, waiting for Buck to stand.

"You hurt her," Buck spat out, his face contorted with hatred. He pushed himself to a kneeling position, fog swirling around his thighs and hands. "I'll take better care of her than you ever could."

Dan's face tightened. "Just leave, you idiot, while you can."

Buck jumped up, holding a heavy branch from the ground. He swung, clubbing Dan's upper arm.

Dan jerked back. Blood oozed, black in the dim light becoming a trickle running down his arm. "Hell, you're persistent." Dan crouched and moved sideways, staying just out of reach.

"Buck, stop," Kari yelled. He ignored her. "Red, red, red!" she screamed at the top of her voice. *Oh, God, somebody. Please come.*

Buck jumped at the sound, then turned his head. Dan slapped the club aside and slammed a fist into his face, then punched him in the stomach, folding him over. Bringing his hands up, he caught Buck's jaw and tossed him backward. The man hit the ground hard.

Relief flooded Kari. *Thank you, thank you, thank you.* She released the breath she'd been holding.

Master Nolan burst into the clearing, skidded to a stop. His glance flickered over Kari, Dan, and then Buck. He shook his head. "Didn't know you were into ménages," he said in a dry voice.

Dan snorted. Frowning down at his arm, he shook his head in disgust. "I'm getting slow."

Kari had moved to help him when Master Z appeared. He put an arm around her and pulled her against his side. "Are you hurt, little one?"

"I'm all right." She attempted a laugh. "I even got a kick in."

"Indeed."

As Master Nolan tied something around the gash on Dan's arm—a silk cloth he probably used for restraints—Kari took a step forward, wanting to make sure Sir was all right. She stopped herself. He didn't want her. She had to remember that.

Dan rubbed his jaw, glanced at the makeshift bandage. "Thanks."

"No problem." Nolan nudged Buck with his foot and got a groan. "I'll even take the garbage out."

Master Dan motioned to Kari. "Let's get you out of here before anything else happens. I'll find someone to take you home."

She considered arguing. Could they maybe talk this out? Then she shrugged. What was the point?

He put his hand against her lower back, the warmth against her bare skin reminding her she was naked. "Let's go."

Master Z and Nolan came behind them, half dragging the stunned Buck.

Just before they reached the door of the mansion, Master Z called, "Kari, I want to speak to you. Dan, please help Nolan with this idiot."

Master Z stepped to one side so Dan could take Buck's other arm. As the men moved away, Kari joined Z in the shadows.

Z studied her face. "Did the violence leave you shaken?"

"Not really. Not now." She looked at her hands. Not even a tremble. "I've seen fighting. I teach high school, and I swear there's a brawl or two every lunch period."

He chuckled. "No wonder you kept your head so well." He turned his head to watch the men. Another DM ran out to help with Buck. "Do you still want Dan?"

The unexpected question shocked her, and a wave of longing welled up in her, tied her tongue.

"Well, that emotion is clear enough; you definitely want him." Smiling, he rubbed his knuckles over her cheek. "He wants you too, Kari, much as he'd like to deny it. And between your walking away and then Buck wanting you back, his defenses have been shaken. But if he goes home now, he'll shore them back up."

"What can I do?" she asked, frowning at Sir's broad back as he handed Buck over to the other men.

"Kitten, if you run, he'll chase you. He won't be able to help himself after fighting another man for you. Once he catches you..." Z sighed and shook his head. "I can't predict how he'll react at that point."

He'd catch her. Probably be pretty angry too. She bit her lip. "He'd never hurt me. Not in anger."

"You know him well then." Z tilted his head and waited.

He might hurt her heart, though. Again. The jerk. "I'll do it. Who knows, maybe Master Nolan will catch me first."

He barked a laugh. "You've got a mean streak, little one. Go now while you have a head start."

CHAPTER SEVENTEEN

Having disposed of the asshole, Dan walked back out into the Gardens. He felt strange. Lighter. Probably from pounding on Buck. A fight was a damn good way to unload emotion. He'd enjoyed the hell out of planting his fist in the guy's gut. God knew he'd needed to punch someone and—his step stalled—and Marion wasn't around to yell at. Much of that anger he'd expended had been at her.

But he wasn't angry anymore. How could he be? She'd paid horribly for her mistake. Oddly enough, his guilt had disappeared with the anger. Someday, he'd have to thank Kari.

But right now, he wanted to take her home. He might feel better, but he still had no intention of getting involved or... He frowned. Z stood alone in the shadows of the trees. "Where's Kari?"

"Went back in." Z jerked his head at the Gardens.

"What the hell do you mean she went in? You let her go back in the Gardens?"

Z shrugged. "She wanted to play some more. Said maybe Nolan would find her before you."

"Did she now?" Nolan walked up behind Dan. "Guess I'll have to—"

Dan growled. "You take one fucking step farther, and I'll take you apart."

The corner of Nolan's mouth tipped up, and Dan let out a breath. Hell of a lot of control he was showing. "Sorry, Nolan."

But hearing that asshole Buck say he'd take better care of her, when Dan had been trying to find her to apologize, and now to have Nolan doing the same...

"I'll go get her," he told Z. "And then I'll beat her ass for a while."

"Indeed."

Her curved bottom, soft under his hand. Her mouth quivering. Her eyes warming at the sight of him. "I'll find her," he repeated.

She ran.

One corner, then another. He was going to be... The word *annoyed* wasn't nearly descriptive enough. The thought increased Kari's speed. Her glow-sticks shone too brightly, beacons in the eerie fog. She whipped around a fountain, circling toward the right. How had she let Master Z goad her into this?

She shook her head, knowing the answer. Stupid Kari. How many times was she going to let him hurt her?

At the right corner of the Gardens in a wide clearing, the grass hadn't yet been cut. The cool strands brushed over the top of her feet. She slowed and dropped to her knees. If she sat on her ankles, only a faint gleam from her ankle bracelet escaped through the higher strands. She tucked her glowing wrist between her legs and scowled when the light lit her pale skin faintly pink. But if he didn't get too close, he wouldn't see it.

He wasn't the only one in a bad mood after all, and she felt like making him work a little.

From the right, a man shouted in victory. Kari hunched closer to the ground. A panting fight from another direction ended in a woman's shriek and a man's rumbled satisfaction. The minutes passed. Her legs started to cramp.

Had he given up? Maybe he didn't even want her, hadn't even come after her at all.

Then she saw a thin pink light moving steadily closer, flickering through the intervening bushes.

She could hear him now, his footsteps even and slow. Stalking her. Her heart started to hammer, her fingers closing around strands of grass. He wouldn't hurt her; her head knew that, but her body...her body felt like prey and wanted to run.

Closer. He knew she was hiding for he checked each small clearing. Her area came next. *Oh, God.* Her nerve broke. She scrambled to her feet and darted away.

He gave a grunt of satisfaction. Heavy footsteps thudded behind her. Risking a glance back, she saw him, bare chested and heavily muscled with the determined, cruel face of a predator.

Ignoring caution, she ran faster.

He closed on her. Out of breath, she stumbled, her heart hammering so loud she couldn't hear him. His hand closed on her arm, pulling her around. She yanked, and his hand slipped off.

She sprinted away. Glancing back, she saw he'd disappeared. She slowed.

He charged her from the side, huge and overpowering, bringing them both down onto the grass. He rolled at the last minute, taking the fall on his back, protecting her with his arms.

Panting for breath, she fought him instinctively, still covered in enough oil that his grip couldn't hold her. She kicked at him, and he laughed. His hard hands slid over her breasts, her waist. She slid free and pushed to her feet.

He grabbed her ankle and yanked her down on top of him. Rolling, he pinned her under him, his weight inescapable.

She squirmed frantically as he flipped her onto her stomach, sitting on her as he loosened his leathers, applied a condom. She tried to crawl away as his implacable hands hauled her onto her knees, his arm securing her in place.

Fingers parted her folds, probing, sliding into her, her wetness a stunning betrayal.

A second later, he rammed into her, burying himself so hard, she cried out in shock. She tried to crawl away from the impaling shaft and from the treacherous pleasure.

"God, no, sweetheart. You're not getting away." His fingers dug into her hips, holding her immovable as he hammered into her, over and over. "You're mine, Kari," he growled. "My sub. My woman. Mine." Each word was punctuated by a hard thrust.

He'd called her his woman? A thrill ran through her. *But it wasn't true*. Shaking her head frantically, she tried to pull away.

With a low snarl, he shoved her knees farther apart and lifted her bottom higher, rendering her more helpless.

As she strained against the grip of his big hands, arousal shot through her, every nerve in her body flaming to life. His thick shaft plunged in and out of her sensitive tissues ruthlessly, and she tightened around him, the need becoming unbearable. She keened, unable to stop the sound.

A ripple started inside her, like a tidal wave, carrying everything before it, intensifying until she convulsed around him, until her whole body shook with the strength of the exquisite spasms, her voice lifting in high cries of bliss.

And then he buried himself deep, deep inside her and came with a low roar.

Her arms gave out, and she landed on her forearms, dropping her heavy head in the grass. He still held her hips in the air, breathing in heavy gasps.

She felt battered inside and out. Taken. Possessed. His words rang in her ears. "*My sub. My woman. Mine.*"

. . .

Dan's words rang in his ears. "*My sub. My woman. Mine.*"

Her body trembled in his grip, her pussy giving intermittent twitches of satisfaction. He'd used her hard, reacting to Buck's attack and her taunting like the alpha he was. He'd had to possess her, to brand her with his scent, his body, his cum.

Mine.

He couldn't move. His fingers wouldn't release their grip on her soft hips.

He didn't want to release her. Ever. No matter how often his mind told him to retreat from her, his emotions and his body kept forcing him back.

His own expression came back to him. "*Your body likes that idea,*" he'd told her, trying to teach her to look past her inhibitions. Hadn't done a hell of a job following his own advice, had he? He'd been too busy looking to the past.

She'd hit him over the head with the truth, shown him he was both blind and deaf, and then she'd walked away.

He'd already been coming after her when the asshole attacked. Dan's jaw tightened. Should have punched the bastard a few more times, loosened some teeth.

Then again, maybe he should have thanked him. All-unknowing, the asshole had finished the awakening of Master Dan, the biggest idiot on the planet. But his ears were open now, and his body was telling him that he'd found his mate.

His heart agreed.

Beat a man over the head hard enough, and he'll eventually figure things out.

Dan leaned forward and pressed a kiss to the nape of his little sub's neck. Slowly he pulled out of her. The whimper as she was emptied made him smile. He patted her soft ass. "I'll be right back, sweetheart." He disposed of the condom.

When he returned, she let him pull her into his arms, all her fight fucked right out of her. That shouldn't have felt so gratifying. With a sigh, she snuggled close like a milk-fed puppy. Having her there, fitting against him as if she'd been designed for him... his world seemed to jerk and spin and suddenly right itself. Yeah, she was his.

Now all he had to do was get her to agree to take on a cynical cop with a penchant for kinky sex.

Piece of cake.

Kari rubbed her cheek against Sir's skin, wanting to take his scent with her when she left. And she needed to leave. Now. Before she burrowed farther into his arms. Why had Master Z thought Sir chasing her would make a difference? Why had she even tried? He'd used her and now held her...just like every other time. Had she really thought he'd blurt out some romantic nonsense?

She had to get out of here. At the thought of standing up and walking away *again*, she wanted to cry. "Let me go, please." She pushed away from his body. "I'm going home. I want you to leave me alone."

"No, you don't." He pulled her closer, his fingers tightening on her hip like a steel trap. "Did you hear me say you're mine?"

Just hearing the words tugged at her heart. And yet, in a minute, he'd turn that cold face on her. "Just now?" she said, trying for a polite, indifferent tone.

"Mmmmh, just now when I was buried so deep inside you I never wanted to leave."

The rumbling words made her shiver. Still, she knew what came next. She struggled up and braced herself with a forearm across his chest. She'd take the news looking at him, not huddling like a child.

His hand cupped her cheek. "I meant that, sweetheart. You're mine." He smiled slowly, his cheek creasing. "And I intend to keep you."

"Keep me?" Her heart bounced inside her, choking her words into incoherence.

His eyes were intent, and she realized he'd been studying her face. A satisfied smile crossed his lips.

"You can't keep me."

"Oh, but I can." His finger traced her lips, and the look in his eyes was one she hadn't seen before. "Your body says it likes the idea."

Keep her? She shoved the hope down. *Don't be silly*. He meant he'd see her at the club, use her as a sub. "You mean here at the club?"

"Here, Kari. And everywhere else."

Her brows drew together. There had to be a catch. "Does that mean I get to keep you also?"

"Oh, absolutely." He kissed her, his lips demanding. "I'm a firm believer in equality at all times—"

"At all times?" She glanced at the cuffs clipped to his leathers. "Why do I find that hard to believe?" And why the heck was she arguing with him. *Mine, mine, mine*.

"At all times," he repeated. "However, in the bedroom or in the club, I am a lot more equal than you." His grin flashed white before he rolled her onto her back. Pinning her between his knees, he buckled her cuffs on.

"Jerk," she said, the joy impossible to contain.

"That would be me. But I'm *your* jerk." He lifted her hands over her head, trapped them there. Leaning down, he stopped with his mouth an inch away from hers, his breath warm on her face. "We'll discuss this later, but you're at the club right now. So what do you say to me, little sub?"

She barely managed to whisper, "Yes, Sir," before he took her mouth and kissed any thought of defiance right out of her head.

ALSO BY CHERISE SINCLAIR

Masters of the Shadowlands Series

Club Shadowlands

Dark Citadel

Breaking Free

Lean on Me

Make Me, Sir

To Command and Collar

This Is Who I Am

If Only

Show Me, Baby

Servicing the Target

Protecting His Own

Mischief and the Masters

Beneath the Scars

Defiance

The Effing List

It'll Be An Adventure

Mountain Masters & Dark Haven Series

Master of the Mountain

Simon Says: Mine

Master of the Abyss

Master of the Dark Side

My Liege of Dark Haven

Edge of the Enforcer

Master of Freedom

Master of Solitude

I Will Not Beg

The Wild Hunt Legacy

Hour of the Lion

Winter of the Wolf

Eventide of the Bear

Leap of the Lion

Healing of the Wolf

Heart of the Wolf

Sons of the Survivalist Series

Not a Hero

Lethal Balance

What You See

Soar High

Standalone Books

The Dom's Dungeon

The Starlight Rite

ABOUT THE AUTHOR

Cherise Sinclair is a *New York Times* and *USA Today* bestselling author of emotional, suspenseful romance. She loves to match up devastatingly powerful males with heroines who can hold their own against the subtle—and not-so-subtle—alpha male pressure.

Fledglings having flown the nest, Cherise, her beloved husband, an eighty-pound lap-puppy, and one fussy feline live in the Pacific Northwest where nothing is cozier than a rainy day spent writing.

Printed in Great Britain
by Amazon